Loaves of Bodies

Baked by the sun
a roast of destinies
afloat on liquid skin
Puffed up like dough for a bite by fishes
tossed relentless by the waves
Regurgitated
yielding no mastication
until aground lifeless by the shore

EVARISTUS AGBISONG BASSEY

Published by

Green Hillz Books

Oban Green Hillz 41B Kabusa Gardens Estate Abuja FCT
Nigeria

Copyright © **Evaristus A. Bassey, 2019**

No part of this book may be republished, reprinted, distributed,
without the author's permission.

ISBN 978-978-57318-7-3

To A New Nigeria

GRATITUDE

To all I encountered in any way that enriched these stories, my heart goes in gratitude. I am grateful to my Archbishop Joseph E. Ekuwem who granted me sabbatical leave after eight years of service at Caritas Nigeria, during which time I wrote these stories. I am also grateful to Canon Seamus at St. Joseph's, Bedford, United Kingdom, who accommodated me for several weeks, along with Frs Joe Udo and Patrick Udotai, friends of mine who hosted me severally in the UK, as well as Fr. Ben Okon who hosted me in Turin, Italy. I am grateful to Pamela McNally in the UK whose feedback was quite encouraging, and Adesuwa Iluobe who also read and gave me very good feedback. To my bosom friends and brothers Emmanuel Ntuyang and Joe Edet - with whom I had to attend a refresher course at the Goldsmith University of London, whose encouragement is ever enduring, I remain very grateful. Particularly to Almighty God, for the continuous gift of the priesthood, unworthy as I am, I am eternally grateful.

CONTENTS

LOAVES OF BODIES

BOOK ONE

A VERY DECENT MAN

1.

He had never hit on a girl in his entire life and yet was married with three kids!

He got married to his wife because the priest opened his eyes. He had taken a liking to the priest, a young urbane man of 28 years of age who was already having a receding hairline and smiled with the most beautiful dimples. He was only two years as a priest and his contemporary somewhat. He and Ono and a few other guys and girls often crowded round the priest after mass on Sunday because he was simply a jolly good fellow and he would invite them back to the parish on a certain evening to accompany him to take communion to the sick, or assist him in praying for the many intentions people forwarded to him. He would say "I want to pray for so and so please join me for half an hour" and it would turn into an hour or so because he would bring out the Blessed Sacrament and expose it for them to worship and make intercessions. He would often say praying without the BS as he casually abbreviated it was like eating bread without butter or jam.

On one occasion therefore, he went to see Fr Itanja or Fr Ja as they called him and confided in him that he had started praying for a wife. He wanted Fr Ja to join in his intention but privately so that he would not be mocked by others. To his amazement Fr Ja refused.

"Pray for what? It's a waste of my time. I don't pray for things that are obvious."

"Obvious? How do you mean Father?" He asked completely taken aback, his face frozen. Gabe had this smile that was often affixed on his face as his default countenance which made him part his large lips unconsciously. Sometimes he even breathed through his mouth. He batted his eyes severally as someone waking up from sleep and drew himself completely together defacing the smile. His friends teased him that God made a mistake endowing him with luscious lips and big eyes for nothing. He closed his mouth as he stared at Fr Ja in complete surprise.

"Do you want a woman to drop from heaven for you to marry? What of Ono? Is she a man? I thought you two were friends?"

"Ono?" And that was how his mouth remained agape as Fr Ja continued to sort out things from his car apparently done with the issue. "We are just friends, me and Ono," he managed to find his voice. "Nothing between us."

"So, you want an enemy to marry? See Ono there. Look at her very well. Isn't she wife enough?"

Ono was chatting away with a group of young men and women at a distance. He forced a look at her, realizing instantly that Fr Ja was right. She was not exactly short but then she was not that tall. She passed for those girls you would correctly refer to as cute. She was petite in a romantic kind of way and had this boisterous laughter that would make you laugh because she was laughing even if you did not know why she was laughing. She was not heavily endowed in her bosom but she compensated for those with her bum which was always obvious because of her well fitted dresses.

He Gabriel had even foolishly discussed severally with Ono about the kind of woman he would want to marry and sought her help to pray about it. He had attended a coed and could relate perfectly freely with a girl without considering her sexuality. And that was how he had related with Ono all along. Girls were more used to having boys as friends without considering their sexuality so Ono herself did not make any assumptions since she had not been asked to be girlfriends or something. Besides among the inner circle that milled around Fr Ja who joined him at his special prayers, they considered themselves holy and tried to live above board. But what Fr. Ja said that evening shook off the scales and brought everything together in one piece, the way a pet owner who had escaped being pounced upon by his lion realized they weren't blood relatives. Ono was a woman after all and a beautiful one at that and it was Fr Ja that had helped open his eyes to see that. He had been looking for an imaginary bride when there was one right beside him. That evening, Fr Ja was not done with his drama. He beckoned on Ono who came over.

"Gabe wants to marry you," he said in a matter of fact manner.

Ono laughed heartily and said. "Fr Ja you can't be serious. He is only my friend. This one has no money even to eat o. You can't be serious Fr." She laughed. But then she noticed no one was laughing along with her.

"I see. So, you guys look out for who your enemies are to marry. Ok o. Go and look for your enemies na not your friends." At this point they both laughed. "Anyway. You may not see what I see. Let us pray about it. Think along those lines and if it doesn't work out you move on. It is not money that marries, it's two human beings ready to commit to each other. Let's put it in God's hands." Right there he held each of their hands and prayed that God might open the eyes of their minds.

That was how it happened, as if the clouds dispersed and an evening sun shone brightly on the gloom and parted it like a huge stage curtain that reveals the long-awaited performance. They already knew each other. They knew what made the other laugh and what brought a tear. They realized they already loved each other and only awaited an ignition, and Fr. Ja had joined the cable ends for the explosion. That is how he took Ono to his village and introduced her to his parents and to other members of his family. His parents later accompanied him to Ntebachot, Ono's village and they did the traditional rites after six months of engagement. It was during that traditional engagement ceremony that he gave her an engagement ring. Six months later, after weekly marriage counseling sessions they were wedded, he a fresh graduate preparing for law school and Ono a fresh midwife, both of them virgins! No savings. No regular income on his part, except for commissions he got from marketing laptop computers. And they had not been afraid to make it!

At first, he suggested they wait and make some money before they settled down. Besides he sympathized with Ono who as a lady would want a fabulous wedding. Weddings were always a woman's thing, a memorable day to show off and an eternal memorial, a day to make friends wish they were in her place, and the more fantastic, the better. But Ono surprised him and suggested they not even print cards. "Since essentially, we are giving ourselves to each other with the church as witness, does it matter if we officially invite anyone or not?" Anyway, in their part of the world, whether someone received a card or not, once they knew about such an event and they knew you, they felt obliged to attend. So, they ended up not printing cards and chose the beautiful chapel at the Holy Child convent across the parish church and had the wedding with mainly close family members in attendance, with one of the parish choirs leading in the singing, along with a few altar servers and altar girls who had done the decoration. The reception was held at the same convent gardens. What was touted in their minds to be a nondescript wedding turned out to be a highly exclusive romantic happenstance. The arrangement of the white pleated chairs and purple tables, spread around the flowers, the cool garden lights – as it was timed to end towards the evening, made everything so beautiful that you would think two stars had a get-away celebration. The truth came home to him that one did not need a crowd to be happy, to be wedded, to love. Because they had not spent so much effort preparing for the vain things, they had been more relaxed assimilating the other significances. He had witnessed situations where all the couple did was plan for the wedding and never for the marriage and when the last guests left it dawned on them that all they had was themselves and yet they had not really learnt to be a gift to each other. But his own case was different. They danced and danced that night until everyone was tired and the disc jockey they hired for the evening was ready to close shop. They left to their hotel room that night around 10 pm.

He could still remember how he struggled that night to penetrate. He tried to no end to break the hymen until Ono patted him at the back and asked him to relax. She knew it was his first time too. She had at least smooched severally in the past but had never allowed any man to penetrate because she wanted it to be her husband's privilege. He was already feeling like a failure, incompetent. How could a man fail to deflower his own wife! It wasn't a rape, you had all the time in the world and yet failed. Haba!

"Promise me something," Ono said to him that night as she sat up and looked into his eyes. His heart suddenly cut and pounded faster. Maybe she saw the fear in his face, she said. "Don't worry about this night. We will make it up. We have our whole lives. I will look for some lubricants tomorrow to ease the job." And typically of women, she often used that to tease him as the man who was given the meat rapists craved for and could not move an inch and he would laugh in that vulnerable way in which every man is a boy and husband to the woman who was both wife and mother. "Promise me that you will be more than money to me."

He was taken aback. More than money!

"Honey. You know I would promise you anything that I could. But this money thing. I didn't even know I was money. I don't even have it so how am I Mr. Money in the first place?" And that became his other appellation. Mr. Money. And he would call her Mrs.

Money. And he found that in all these years to retain meaning, one way was taking something off the cuff and turning it into a joke, a matter for a mild taunt even if it was just between the two that had become one.

"You know I grew up with my sister. The husband was very well to do. He was a contractor. Then a new government came and terminated all the relationships and even refused to pay for what had been done before. I saw my brother-in-law lose his manhood. At some point my sister became the breadwinner and I couldn't believe the toxicity that developed between them afterwards. My sister would make the money, provide for the house and yet she won't have peace."

"Isn't that because whenever the woman becomes the bread winner she now wants to sit on the man's head?"

"On the contrary. What I learnt from my brother-in-law was that he saw himself as money. He saw love as money. Marriage was money to him. And so, when the money finished he was finished and so did the love and marriage."

"But didn't your sister trigger his toxic behavior?"

"Not at all. My sister did all she could to reassure him. She tried her best to remain a loving and respectful wife. It was when the burden was too much on my sister and all he did was sit at home and watch TV all day not assisting my sister in any way domestically; he would eat, drink and leave everything there in the living room for my sister to come back from work and clear. My sister would encourage him to go out and search for jobs. At a point he even had an offer to work at a government ministry but he turned it down because the money was 'too small' and yet the salary would have been higher than my sister's. Then he started blaming her for everything. He would harp on a little matter from night till morning."

"I suppose it is not easy for a man not to provide for the house."

"The man brings the money and expects the woman to be at his service. But when it is the woman that brings the money she does not turn the man into a slave, she requires the man to be supportive at least, to make effort to take back his position. I think what broke my sister down was that he made no effort at all and did not appreciate all her sacrifices. If all that matters is you and me we will know that in good times or bad times we are stuck together, no unnecessary airs."

He considered that for a moment. She was making a lot of sense. These were matters couples hardly talked about in their early years of marriage so that it could become a sort of guidance for the future. He was glad she was bringing up these issues.

"But do you know that it is easier for a woman to regain some income if she loses her job than the man? I mean in our African context, a woman could fry bean cakes and sell, she could sell peanuts or cook food and go to construction sites and sell and not feel socially discriminated. But a man's options are limited."

"I know. But at least the man could hang around the construction site in case additional hands are needed. I believe that so long as it is a legitimate means, no one should be ashamed of making money. In fact, that is the money that is valuable to our hearts, hard earned money. Anyway, all I want you to promise is that you, not your money will be there for me always because your money might finish but I don't want you to deplete, to finish." And it became another barometer in all the years. He would ask "Am I depleting?" And she would say no. Or out of the blue she would say "You are depleting" and he would know it was a jocular way of saying he was a bit off of the union. And so that night, once more he said "I do." And he held her, kissed her and attempted again to penetrate but she said it was painful. "It doesn't always have to take place on the wedding night you know," she said.

2.

That was twenty-five years ago and three children by the side. Now he was a dysfunctional 53-year-old who felt terrible at not being able to make love to his wife anymore. Ono would tease him and say "If you were not the father of these my children I would have said you had never had an erection." And she would laugh in that way in which she turned everything into a joke. He knew what she was trying to do. She wanted to let him know she was not worried so he too should not. Of course, he laughed too but secretly it gnawed at his core and began to chip away at his confidence. At some point Ono asked him why he was so worried. "Is it not just you and me? And we know ourselves," she said rolling her eyes in an attempt to reassure him. And that precisely was what he wanted, for her to have to roll her eyes not over a memorial.

He was worried that he may have become impotent. This was already running into the sixth month and each attempt had ended with a very weak erection that he had to give up altogether. What worried him now was a side comment Ono made. "Perhaps I am no longer attractive," and laughed walking off. She did not know she had stung him too hard for words. Was that true? Was she no longer attractive? To him? It was when she told him two weeks later about a pass a colleague had made to her that he realized the dysfunction also had an effect on her. She confessed that she followed up to know he wasn't flattering her and when she realized he was serious, she put him on check, that the encounter gave her some assurances that she was still a beautiful woman. "Even if my husband doesn't find me beautiful anymore other men find me attractive."

"So now you want to follow other men?"

"I didn't say that. I was only telling you about my own fears and how I dealt with them. Deal with yours. You are depleting." And she laughed in that wild way which made him chase after her and catch up with her. In those days he would have dragged her to the bedroom and made love to her but as he held her hand his confidence waned, his heart began to beat faster than usual. Thankfully it was their daughter that saved the day. She bumped into them on the corridor just then. "Are you two never tired of each other! I don't want any brother or sister again o. Old people behaving like teenagers," she said with a sneer. She was thirteen and very insolent.

"Shut up. You this girl. Go and do your homework," Ono said. He breathed a sigh of relief and pinned her against the wall and smooched her. One thing they could boast about was that the children never found them abusing each other. Early in their marriage they had agreed on a fine. If anyone was responsible he or she alone would do the chores while the other watched. Apart from the bedroom, the other spot their love was most expressed was the kitchen. Even if he had nothing to do he would stand by or sit around giving support. He would be the errand boy. When their first child grew up enough to help in the kitchen Ono suggested he stop but he insisted that he was already used to it and would feel as if he was missing something. Many times, they were the subject of gossip for the children. "I caught daddy kissing mum in the kitchen..." "Don't mind those two." They enjoyed being caught too. They wanted their children to grow up in an atmosphere of love, to show that it was possible for a husband and wife to be romantically in love, that love was actually a matter of acts of daily commitments and even when you felt low sometimes you could high up by an immediate decision.

An awkward moment was about to set in when Ono dragged him to the room.

"Okay let's talk about this again." She said. She collected his phone. "Thank God for google. Nowadays you can find out anything you want to know. Let's look at erectile dysfunction together." The site took them to a short survey of ten questions and the answers they both checked gave an ED Score of 18. 1-7 was Severe;8-11 Moderate to Severe; 12-16 Mild to Moderate while 17-21 was Mild.

"So, you see, it is a little matter. You are the one taking it as a big issue. Relax. We need to check your BP again and do fasting blood sugar to be sure it is none of those things. Meanwhile just calm down."

His phone rang.

He took it from her. It was Ekuri. He was hesitating.

"You won't pick your call?" She snatched the phone and said "Hello. Ekus. How far na," she said, speaking in pidgin English.

"Our Madam. How you dey? Where your Oga? Tell am say I dey wait for am o."

She handed him the phone.

"Ol Boy. I no sure say I go fit come out o," he said, trying to cancel the engagement.

"My friend. Who want sit here alone chop fish. Oya begin dey come now now."

"Go now," Ono urged him. "Go and join your friends if that would calm you down. I know you are not really yourself."

"He wants us to sit out and I don't really feel like it."

"If you agreed to it earlier why do you want to change your mind? See how woman dey sweet you. Oya come and go out." She said it playfully. At first her words struck at his conscience. *See how woman dey sweet you.* Was it not James Hadley Chase that wrote a book entitled *The Guilty Are Afraid?* Of course, the woman she was referring to here was herself and it was good she still saw herself that way, as still having such an effect on her husband that he could cancel a sit out with a friend just to be with her. She truly thanked God for Fr Ja who opened their eyes to each other for she had never known what true love was other than what this her husband gave to her, and it was such an idyllic union, everyday longing to be home to see each other. Even when the children started coming and it seemed that her attention was being taken from him, he managed to snuggle in and make it both their responsibility so that at no time did he feel abandoned because of the children. She was a happy woman because she knew she had her husband's attention any day anytime.

See how woman dey sweet you... On the flip side she was

being prophetic because he was actually going out because of a woman. He had become so anxious about the ED issue that two weeks ago Ekuri or Ekus as they called him saw through him and said he looked like someone with a problem. He had prodded him until he talked about it. Ekus was one of his close pals but they hardly hung out because he was either in church for a program or just plain tired at home. Ekus confided in him that his wife didn't really know how to cook well, so sometimes he would call him up and ask for when he was having lunch. He had told Ono about this and she was quite pleased that his friend admired her culinary abilities. Sometimes he would even ask Ekus to go to his home and be served a meal. Ekus had asked whether the erectile dysfunction happened only with his wife or with other women as well.

"What do you mean other women? Am I supposed to be sleeping with other women?" he queried him.

"Come on man. We are friends. You don't have a girlfriend?"

"That is ridiculous. Why should I have a girlfriend when I am married!"

"Ok sir. No vex," Ekuri said, seeing the genuine surprise on Gabe's face. "But come Old Boy. Are you serious? You no get girl?"

"I no get."

"You no get for now or you never do any other person apart from Wifey?" He was looking at him in great surprise. "Talk true. Swear."

"Swear for wetin na. I say I never do."

"For twenty-five years? O'Boy you be Angel Gabriel o. Ok. No be say I want you to get girlfriend because that comes with responsibilities and could drag your attention especially if you are a novice. Wifey fit catch you sef. So listen to me." So Ekuri plotted it all out. He would arrange a girl for him, a good girl, as in not one infested with any transmittable diseases, he wouldn't need to keep her as girlfriend, he just had to do it with her to assure himself that there was nothing wrong with him. He would then know that perhaps there was something a bit off in his relationship with his wife and could work on it.

After several days of talking him into it he gradually wormed himself into the plot.

And this was the day.

"Carry some money o," Ekuri warned him that day.

"Is she a prostitute?"

"Kai mennn. You are so naïve. So, you will come, chop woman finish, you waka go home without dropping something? You need a whole education. Your wife wey you dey give money na prostitute ?"

"Leave my wife out of this. She is my wife."

"Ok na. Don't come there with an empty pocket and do holy holy o. I am warning you now. All these fine girls you see around who do you think takes care of them? Dem Papa? Kai. I no fit believe for this 21st Century. Women need money!"

He remembered a conversation he had with Ono about women and money over a twitter post castigating women and their love for money. It was Ono that brought home the clarification. "Well it might seem true that women love money. But I don't think so. A decent girl requires money for hair, cosmetics, toiletries, a change of clothes which a boy may not require. Some parents have not taught their wards to be modest so you find some who go to the extreme. I don't think girls sleep with any man and accept money, that would make them prostitutes. I for one couldn't accept any man's money but I like my husband's money." So, they concluded that though women didn't really love money, they liked their men's money. He had married when he was not that exposed, and as it is a fact that women mature earlier than men, even though he was five years older than Ono, she was the one that taught him many things and brought him out of his naivety. His closed associations also had not helped matters and he knew that generally he was seen as a 'holy' man; even colleagues were controlled in the kinds of jokes they expressed around him. He was simply a very decent man. And now he had to go out to meet a good girl who would receive money from him after their interaction even though she was not a prostitute.

"Did you shower this evening?" Ono asked him.

"No. Why?"

"Babe quickly shower before you go out so that you feel fresh and then change into something more casual."

3.

Thirty minutes later he drove out. The shower calmed his anxiety somewhat. It was an excellent suggestion because he was smelling all fresh and nice. Ekuri ran a small guest house of ten rooms and had offered Gabe space for the evening to meet the girl in question. He had sent him an SMS that it was Room 090 and that he should go straight to the room without asking questions.

His heart was pounding as he opened the door.

It was the longest thirty minutes. He thought of calling his wife to tell her he had arrived but thought better of it. It wasn't like a journey out of state or something. Ekuri had told him the girl would arrive a few minutes later but he had waited a whole half hour.

She didn't even knock. He saw the handle turn and stood up to help with the door. She walked in and said "Hi" and went straight to the fridge. "I hope there is water here. I am very thirsty." Luckily there was a complimentary bottle of water which she took out and gulped quickly. "Ah ha. Thank God."

She threw the bottle on the floor and went over to the bed and sat down. She tried to take off her pair of jeans trousers and got hooked at the leg opening. It was a very tight pair of stretch jeans. "Help me," she said, waking him to the reality before him. He rushed down and yanked the pair of tight trousers from her feet. He often wondered why the Americans called it pants. She unbuttoned and pulled off her top and was then left with her inner wears. "Let me quickly shower," she said and rushed into the bathroom. She came out minutes later completely naked, went to her hand bag and brought out a body spray, applied some cream and went over to the bed and tucked herself under the sheets. The room was air-conditioned. "Your perf is nice," she said. He stood for an awkward moment and then sat on the edge of the bed. Everything was happening so fast.

"I am Gabe. What's your name ?"

"Yenny."

"Nice to meet you Yenny. I am a lawyer."

"Ok."

"Are you from this state ?"

"No."

"You are a student ?"

"No."

"But you live in town ?"

"Yes."

An awkwardness crept into the room. He noticed that she had started becoming somewhat shy as he was still fully dressed whereas she was completely naked under the sheets. She turned and faced the wall and said almost in a whisper. "Oga you sabi ask question for Africa."

"I'm sorry."

Obviously she considered her life private. She did not want to share details about herself but was willing to expose and even share her most private parts? Was not it only civil to get to know each other first, establish some relationship before getting intimate? Ekuri had asked him to bring a condom but he brushed it aside knowing there was no way he would meet and sleep with a girl who was not a prostitute the same day. That could never happen. Sex was an extremely intimate thing and no woman gave up herself just like that to a man without first flaunting her value. So it was shocking when he saw her emerge from the bathroom completely naked and go under the sheets.

"The lights are affecting my eyes," she said. He went and put them off as there was no bedside switch. The room was dark but for the glow from the television which she had changed the channel to a musical one. The volume was out completely. She brought out her phone and started playing from a playlist.

He slipped into the sheets. It was really becoming dense. First, he pulled his trousers. Then his Tee shirt. He was left with his under wear. By this very act of going under the sheets he knew he had consented to adultery even if he did not penetrate. He debated in his mind whether lying down here as he was equaled to the actual act of doing it.

As he went over these things in his mind he suddenly said. "I am not sleeping here o."

"Who wan sleep here sef. You no wan sleep here and you dey ask plenty questions." She hissed. She now turned towards him with a certain vengeance and grabbed him as if she wanted to teach him a lesson. "You are the shy type. You dey do like say you no like." She laughed. And he laughed too and became more at ease.

A sudden anxiety overcame him. Was this really adultery or an experiment? He tried to talk to himself that all he wanted to know was whether he had become impotent or not. He hadn't set out without any cause to go and look for another woman. It was because he had a challenge and wanted to prove something! It sounded hollow but somewhat reassuring. This would be the first and the last time.

He had some erection as she fondled him but he didn't really have the confidence that it was strong enough to last. This wasn't really his problem as sometimes he could be up but the challenge was maintaining it when he went into his wife because he would shrink a moment later like a lifeless grub found in a dead palm tree. Initially he could even sustain it for many seconds before ejaculating prematurely but it had gradually turned to no erection at all.

"Where is the condom?"

"Huh? Condom? I didn't bring one."

"You did not?" She almost shouted. "What kind of man is this mbok. So, you left your house to come and f*k me without a condom. Let me stand up and go abeg. Which kind thing be dis sef." She stood up quickly looking really upset.

"No. It's not like that," he tried to say. She was already dressing up. He wanted to tell her he hadn't expected them to have sex this first time, that he just wanted to get to know her. But he thought better of it. That might embarrass her. He didn't know where he got the courage but as his embarrassment was much and he didn't want to appear so naïve, he decided to confide in her. "Actually, I have been having issues with my erection. I am happily married. I have never done this. I just wanted to know whether it was strictly my problem or it had a connection with my wife."

"So, I am your guinea pig? You think that because Ekuri has me as girlfriend he is not happily married ?"

"You are Ekuri's girlfriend?"

"Yes na. Him say make I no tell you sha. He told me about your ish and asked me to help you."

He was shocked. He couldn't say a word. "You no get girl friend?"

"No. What for?" He said finding his voice.

"Okay na. But have you had sex before?"

"My Gosh. What kind of question is that? How do you think I had my three kids!"

"No vex oga Gabe. You know sometimes impotent men marry for society sake and allow their wives to conceive from anywhere."

"That is preposterous. God forbid. Nonesense."

"Oga how old you be sef. Have you checked your prostrate and diabetes?"

"That shouldn't be the issue. My sugar level is good and my prostrate though enlarged is not malignant."

"So wetin be the problem na. Abi you get

psychological ish?"

"Is it issue you are calling ish? I don't have."

"Then maybe your wife has an infection."

"What!"

"Oga Gabe. Relax. No be like say she sleep with anyone. It could be a yeast infection which could result from too much sugar or hormonal ish. A woman can have an infection without sleeping with anyone. Me and my boyfriend we cleanse ourselves every six months or so. I am saying this because what you are saying happened between me and my boyfriend."

"Ekuri?"

"No na. I mean my real boyfriend. Ekuri is just a play boy. We only meet for sex. My boyfriend began by having a weak erection and then none whatsoever. I didn't know that my infection was responsible. He would then take treatment and we would have sex once or twice and it would happen again. He had to keep on taking a combination of medicines each time until I dealt with my ish."

"So your ish is gone?"

"Somehow. I saw a special oil online and got it. I just wanted to try it and it worked for me."

"And your real boyfriend never had the ish again??"

"Oga Gabe you sef. Must you add real to boyfriend? Yes o. He never had it again. He is the only one I sleep with without a condom. Maybe you sleep with girls without a condom that is why."

"I already told you. If you must know, I have never used a condom."

"Go away. Lie lie. E get man wey never use condom?"

"True. I have never made love to anyone else than my

wife and I really want to keep it that way. So, you see, I never needed one."

"Hmmm. Na wao. So, people like you still dey waka for this earth? You dey like my boyfriend, the guy good ehn. But him get small side chick and him no know say I know."

"So, he doesn't know about this part of you?"

"Which part Oga Gabe? Na because I come to help you? Me I no be bad girl o. If you see bad girls wetin you go talk? Am I crazy to tell my boyfriend that I do stuff outside? Him no get money na. I get to take care of myself. Him dey give me 25k every month. E dey try sef. But Oga Gabe you sef know say 25K no go anywhere. Only hair and toiletries, the money don finish."

"Hmmm."

"Na Ekus dey help sometimes. Sometimes when some of these guys come into town he links me up so I can get something better."

"Wow. Amazing."

"Wetin dey there sef. Na condom na. You just do it and go your way. Your mind no dey dere. Nothing spoil. No emotion."

"Amazing."

"Seriously I no think say someone like you still dey this Naija o. You no know say just by a click you can have a girl for the night? Only foolish girls stand on the streets. There are girls out there who are lonely, sometimes they don't even need money, they just want someone to f*k them. They don't even want you to know their real names."

"Hmmm. This is a real education for me. You do go to church?"

"Why won't I go to Church? Did God offend me? Na

me offend God so na me get to go beg am. But menn if God wan take sex judge people even pastors no go enter heaven o."

"Let's not talk of men of God."

"Oga Gabe leave that thing. Me I no be child of God? I say for this matter nobody pure. Except Pope. Me I don do many pastors sef. I nearly do Reverend Father sef but I run. I come fear. I advise myself say make I manage other people yet until I upgrade." He sat there perplexed, trying to make sense of everything she was saying. "So, you sef what are you doing with Ekuri as friend? They say show me your friends… Ekuri na pay master o. I dey even arrange my friends give am when I no dey free. Sometimes we dey do troika sef."

"Troika? What's that?"

"Threesome na."

"Threesome…Sorry I don't get."

"Kai oga Gabe. You be real Mugu. You no know wetin be threesome? Like a man having fun with two or three girls at the same time? You no dey watch blue film? You never start life at all. Kai. Na wao. You must be a very boring man."

"Not at all. On the contrary. I have a very happy and exciting life. Can you ever love someone so much that you never think of being with someone else?" He asked her.

"Oga Gabe dat one na JAMB question. I no even believe you sef. Which man wey no dey cheat? Men are all cheats and because of that we have learnt to cheat better. So, as you dey so you think say your wife no get boyfriend?" It was nearly 10pm. The question was rude by all considerations.

"Nonsense. Impossible." He said quite upset. "How

can you even say that about my wife ?"

"You wan bet?"

"Bet what, that my wife has a boyfriend? Nonsense. That is an unthinkable thing." He got incensed. "How can you even say that!"

"Fifty-thousand-naira sir. Give me her details, her WhatsApp number, place of work etc. and I will get back to you in just one week."

"I will give you a hundred thousand naira instead and I will take only twenty from you. Nonsense."

"Oga Gabe calm down o. No be for vexing. We'll see. By the way, let me write the name of the oil for you." He had no pen and paper.

"Why not send it by text message?" He gave her his number.

4.

He offered to drop her off around Zone 6. "Oga Gabe. I see say you be fine man. Anytime you need a girl just call me and I will arrange for you," she said. Somehow it was so funny that he laughed and brought down the tension. He realized she had sent a WhatsApp message to him and wrote the name of the oil. She also asked him to go to a pharmacy and ask for a combination therapy. "Just ask them. They will know," she wrote. "Take that one first before any other treatment. It is a one-day treatment. I am surprised you didn't see a doctor first," she said. Actually he had seen one who asked him to check his BP, fasting blood sugar, do ECG and so on and the results all came out good so he asked if he had anxiety issues and it coincided with when he was duped of some money so the doctor felt it might be that and asked him to calm down and accept the reality of the loss. Otherwise he asked him to try Viagra but he had read stories of how men had heart complications with Viagra and felt he had nothing to prove to anyone and did not take further steps, except the occasional trials and failures with his wife. Six months down the line it had regressed from quick ejaculation to weak erection and practically no erection.

He was hurrying home when he remembered that H-Medix was still open and drove to Wuse ll to enquire about the medicine. "Yes, we have it." They instructed him on how to take it and he bought a bottle of water and took the first tablet straight away. He would take the rest the next morning. He was hungry. He would still have to eat as late as it was. "Your wife's WhatsApp number please." Yenny wrote. He smiled and sent it to her, planning what he would do with the twenty thousand naira bet.

He microwaved his food. Ejama his last girl was still awake watching television. "I need to watch the news please. Are you done with your homework?"

"Yes daddy."

"Okay. Then let's watch the late-night news together since you don't want to go to bed. "

"But I was here first. Go to your room and watch news."

"That will disturb mummy."

"Who told you she is sleeping. That one that will be keeping vigil until you return. She… anyway. I won't tell you."

"Let's see…What time is it? I think the time is Bedtime. See you tomorrow young lady." She stood up and stormed out. He brought up his children in a way that they could express themselves freely while not having a doubt as to who was in charge. "Hey you are forgetting something." She hesitated for a moment and returned to give him a peck on the cheek and said "Good night daddy."

"Goodnight sweet heart. Don't forget to pray your psalms before dozing off." He only did family prayer once a week with the kids on Saturday evening, where they shared the Sunday readings and prayed. He made sure all his children could pray the lauds and the vespers and the compline, using the *iBreviary* application on their phones. Fr. Ja whom he still kept in touch after all these years had made him get used to the psalms having taught them that the prayers were not meant for priests alone. So now with internet acccss everywhere it was so convenient to download and pray. Some evenings he also did catechesis for his children because he considered it his duty to teach his children about the faith. Parishes really had nothing for the young apart from when they were going for First Holy Communion and Confirmation. There was a huge gap in terms of ongoing formation of the people of God while the priests were busy building one physical structure upon another.

He had not seen Ono yet because he hadn't gone inside the room. He guessed what Ejama wanted to tell him was that mummy just stood up to go to the room when he heard his car so she would pretend she was already asleep. Even though he had not really done anything with the girl the mere fact that he slipped under the sheets bothered him. He wanted to gain more control of himself, shed off some guilt before letting her see him.

He brought out a bottle of coke and dumped himself on the sofa. The television was making a noise but he was not aware really of what it was about. His thoughts were on this night, a night of many revelations. It was true he was a real *Mugu*. An idiot. He had been living on the fringes quite unaware of how deep things had become. He had never asked a girl out not just because he was already married but because he did not know how to and did not need to. He imagined that to sleep with a girl you needed to date her, and to date a girl you needed to ask her out, and for a girl to agree to a date, you needed to make several attempts to woo her, which could be quite discouraging. And he already had a ring on his hand, which was an albatross in this regard even if he wanted to. Once at the airport he had felt chatty and sat beside a young lady and one of the first things she said was "Oh. Your wedding ring is beautiful", with a smirk on her face. He got the message. She was telling him 'You are married so don't waste my time.' He had taken the cue and gone ahead to revel her with the story of the ring, how a friend had purchased it in France for them during their tenth anniversary.

"So, this isn't the original wedding ring?"

"No. We were very enthusiastic when we got married so we made do with what we could while planning for a big thanksgiving when we would be ten years old."

"Nice. You seem quite happy talking about your marriage."

"Not just talking about it. I love being married to my wife."

"Oh nice. I hope she feels the same way too."

"Take it from me. She enjoys it more…" and then the flight was called. That had given him the cue that anyone he talked to would first look at his fingers. He did not know that a girl who was not a prostitute could feel so free as to date a man that was married and could strip before a man without any preambles or that a man's girlfriend could agree to sleep with the man's friend and arrange her friends to sleep with the boyfriend in troikas and *perestroikas*! Or that a girl who had agreed to sleep with you could arrange another to do the same. Whenever he had sex with Ono it was so glorious he sometimes praised God in his heart for his wonderful works. He would sometimes shout "Alleluia" if not that he did not consider it appropriate to start praising God in the middle of a sexual activity. And what he treasured so much and held as sacred was what was being hawked without any solicitation. Hmmmm. How did Ekuri do it? How could he appear to love his wife so much and yet sleep around that much? Would his wife still marry him if she knew he was such a 'paymaster' as Yenny called him? As for Yenny, how did she feel sharing her 'man' with her friends? And then her joke about his wife. Did she think that just because she had no moral sense it was same with everyone? He was now regretting why he stepped the bet down to twenty thousand. He should have allowed it remain at one hundred thousand naira to teach her a great lesson.

"I thought you went out to eat fish. Why are you with a plate of food so late in the night?" He wasn't even aware when she walked up and stood behind the couch.

He was flustered. "Honey."

"Apparently you didn't eat the fish."

"No, I did not."

She waited a moment to hear more but he was not forthcoming. In their relationship they had come to agree that instead of telling lies it was better to be silent. Sometimes you just had to say "I don't want to talk about it for now." Although it left the other person wondering, there was more than sufficient trust to carry on. "Maybe it wasn't well cooked or it wasn't your kind of fish?"

"Whatever."

"Ok. I am going off to sleep. I see you want alone time. See you tomorrow."

"Thanks Ono- the- Girl." He called her that sometimes but didn't allow his children to call her that. It was a name that kept her young in his eyes. "Good night."

He turned Netflix on and decided to watch *Gone Girl*. It was a movie with an intricate plot on the extent a woman could go to win back her marriage. It kept him awake till nearly 2am. He had often skipped that movie without knowing the intensity of the plot.

5.

"Hello ma. Good afternoon. I have sent you a Whatsapp message. Please reply."

"Who is this ?"

"My name is Yenny and I need to see you please." The phone went off. Ono quickly went to her message book. It had no name as she didn't have her in her contact list. She promised for the umpteenth time to install true caller on her phone but even so, was it not just the name that true caller gave ? The message was short and direct. "See me if you want to save your marriage. Let's meet at Argungu Restaurant by Jabi Lake Mall by 5pm." And she posted her photo for easy recognition.

She could not wait. Something told her it was serious.

She quickly scanned her activities to see if there was any careless action she had undertaken recently and was satisfied that she had done nothing to injure her marriage. Then it struck her that it might have to do with her husband, maybe about that night. She shrugged. Whatever it was, she was ready for it. Her husband had been a saint practically. He was one in ten million. Even if he messed up one night did not mean he was a bad man.

The four hours were the longest. Her mind went everywhere. She knew she was really up to something and so she went to the venue an hour earlier and waited, ordering boiled vegetables and peppered chicken. At exactly 4.55pm she saw her walk in and signaled to her to join her table.

"What is this all about?" she addressed Yenny a little angrily. "You want to blackmail my husband?"

"Good evening Madam. Finish your food and let us stroll and sit by the lake. I don't want another ear to hear this. Just calm down. You did not even exchange pleasantries. I am not your enemy please. I am even trying to be a friend."

Somehow, she felt she had to be cautious. She finished her meal in silence, carried her bottle of water.

They moved out of the restaurant, as people were trickling in. Usually in the evenings it was a good place to hang out. Sometimes her whole family came out here too.

"Well…Madam. What I am going to tell you will cost you thirty thousand naira." She said as they sat at a corner all by themselves.

"What! You are blackmailing me?"

"Calm down madam. It is not a blackmail. I would be

asking for millions. Listen. I had a bet with your husband. He boasted that you do not have any extramarital affairs and I told him I would check it out and if it was true he would give me fifty thousand or I would give him same if it was not. But he upped it to 100k if it was true and 20k if it wasn't true. As you can see, if I wanted to make money, I could have collected his 100k. So, the 30k I need is to give him his bet prize while 5k is for transport and 5k for the oil I want to give you."

"What oil? I don't do voodoo."

"Calm down madam. I am not talking of voodoo but his erection."

"So, you found out I was cheating? What rubbish is that? How did you and my husband get into that kind of conversation in the first place. Are you his girlfriend?"

"Madam your husband is a very decent man. He has no girlfriend. You sef na decent woman but you dey do small extra ma."

"What does that mean? You are insulting me."

"Madam. Are we going to have a decent conversation or do you really want me to follow my bet through?" She met Ono eyeball to eyeball until she deflected her gaze.

"Fine."

"Good. I am just being plain and nice. I mean no harm to you so let's not escalate things. Let us do it quietly and let things lie. But I will need you to discontinue whatever thing you are doing outside because your man is a very decent man."

"You don't have any evidence. Do you? I need to get home. What oil were you talking about?" She made as if she was gathering herself to leave.

Yenny laughed.

"Madam e be like say you want make I chop your husband's 100k and disgrace you on top. Okay. Let me show you. What surprised me is that you and Ekus set me up with your husband." Ono gave a sigh that came straight from her heart.

"Okay. You win."

"Why don't you delete your messages?"

"What messages ? My phone is pass worded. My husband saw my messages ?"

"Not yet. But he could."

"Not possible. When GSM came we agreed to never look at each other's phones without the other's permission. It was the priest that preached in church that if you are looking for something you will find it, that there was no need going to search messages in our partner's phones because we could misinterpret what we see and a chain of events could start rolling in that may be beyond our control. So, my husband and I resolved to never check each other's phones. He has never checked mine. And I don't even need to check his."

"You sure? Even when you dey sleep him never check your phone?"

"How will I know if I am sleeping? I say he has never checked my phone. He has no need to do that." Just then Ono received a WhatsApp message and it dropped also on Yenny's phone. Yenny checked her phone. "You have a message. Let me read it to you. Check your phone as I read it. 'Can we meet tomorrow for the monthly devotion say by 2pm?' Check it out. That is from Ekus."

"Jeez. What did you do to my phone ? How did you do this? I am finished. I thought they said messages were encrypted end to end and no one else could see your messages. Have you shown my messages to my husband?" She was almost becoming hysterical.

"Relax madam. I am not an enemy. You are drawing attention. Apparently, we are sleeping with the same man. I see also that you are flirting with your colleague and some other young man. You dey hot o. So, you and Ekus are also hitting it out. I thought he was your husband's friend!"

"Is it his enemy I will go and do something with?"

"Orr. No vex madam." Then Ono broke down and started crying softly. "God, I feel sooo bad. My husband is such a nice and innocent man but you know Ekus has flows. I would send him a pic as soon as I got dressed for work and he would praise my dress to high heavens, something my husband would just say "honey you look great." 'Ekus has both sugar, honey and all kinds of sweeteners coated on his tongue. At first, we started flirting on WhatsApp. I hate to say I liked it. I would even look forward to it. Then he would send me suggestive pictures and later on short porn videos. He would tell me how he would take me to high heavens and leave me in eternal bliss. So, it was not difficult when my husband traveled and asked Ekus to come have lunch in the house and deliver some documents he collected from a client. That was before we withdrew our last child from boarding school. I was all alone and he came and had me right there in my sitting room. See understand that I had never experienced any other man in my life, and for the first time I knew what it was to squirt."

"So, it became something regular instead of a one-time experience?"

"Don't make it seem as if I was sleeping with him every day."

"But at least it became a monthly thing. Don't think I am fooled by that monthly devotion thing. Means you were doing it at least once a month. And I guess you had to experience the other two guys as well?"

"I haven't slept with them."

"Yet."

"You are putting words into my mouth."

"So, you fixed me up with your husband!"

"Well. Didn't know it would be you. I saw that my husband was very worried and began to totally lose his confidence so I talked to Ekus about it and he wondered whether he was probably tired of me but would do it with another girl. So, I agreed that he could arrange a girl for him and give me a report later so I know if it was my body he was tired of after twenty-five years."

"So you would have a free for all with Ekus? Anyways. Good news. I didn't f*k him. Apparently, he didn't even come with the intention of doing so because he had no condom with him. I practically had to try and force him but in the end we didn't."

"But did his thing stand?"

"Madam. My hand and your hand no be the same o. My skill no be here. But I have told him what to do. Has he not made love to you since then?"

"The morning after that night, he did. I was surprised. He did watch a movie till late. I was still awake because I was really anxious to see his reaction and whether he would say anything about the night. Usually I lie naked, and it was a bit warm as the current was too low for the air-conditioning. He came and started fondling me and we made love. We did it again later in the night but the thing went weak again subsequently."

"Now here's why I brought the oil. I think you have a recurrent infection which affects his erectile function. Let him treat himself again while you also take the same treatment while using this oil as well. I guarantee you, you will thank me for it. Oya transfer my 30k so I call your husband and tell him to send his account number." Ono did not hesitate. Shortly afterwards Yenny received an alert. "You sent 50k! You are a sweet Mama. Thank you. Oya wait. Let me call your husband." She brought out her ear piece and gave her one to listen into their conversation.

"Hello Oga Gabe."

"Hello. Who's this?"

"Kai. Dis man sef. So, you never store my number. How I go get arrange babe for you na." He laughed heartily.

"Oh Yenny. Good to hear from you. You know I am not cut out for that."

"You sef. Why you no go become reverend father? Your mate dem dey enjoy life you dey do holy holy."

"Yenny you can never know. I have the sweetest life. I have the sweetest woman on earth. So, any news? Are you ready to part with a whooping twenty thousand naira for an unemployed graduate?"

"How you sure say no be you owe me hundred k?"

There was a hearty and long laugh at the end of the line. Ono was momentarily tensed up.

"That is not possible."

"Well Oga. No too trust human being o. Na only God no fit betray our trust. But anyway, I called to ask for your account number. You won. She dey pure."

"I told you so. My wife is an angel. Don't worry about it. Keep the money."

"No Oga Gabe. A bet is a bet. Send me the number let me transfer the cash."

"Don't worry Yenny. I should even pay you for confirming my faith in my wife. I have never doubted her nor will I ever do so, this just makes me love her more. But by the way, how did you do this?"

"I hacked her WhatsApp."

"You did what?"

"I hacked her WhatsApp so I was reading every message that came to her in real time. If she had anything to do outside there's no way she wouldn't have betrayed it after a week. Sorry. I cloned yours too. For instance, an hour ago, you got a message from Ekus and you called him a beast, that how could he send a girl he sleeps with regularly to you…Am I right sir ? And Ekus said 'What if you knew the depths of nothingness?"

"Jeez." They could hear Gabe scream from the other end. "How did you do that?"

"Simple sir and it's not because I studied IT in India and UK."

"You schooled abroad?"

"Yes na Na job I dey look for. I find ways to keep myself entertained."

"Amazing feat. I thought it was all so secure."

"Sir nothing is really secure. If it is secure for a year or two or three someone is going to find a way to break in just to interrogate that notion that it is secure only that it will not be public knowledge. If you want to hack into anyone's WhatsApp all you need do is download Mobiletrackerfree.com. I can show you how to do it from Play store where you uncheck Play

Protect, go to WI FI and click accept, grant all the permissions, accept mobile tracker, create an account, enable accessibility, click on instant messaging and then click the WhatsApp option, and voila, all the messages in real time are on your phone as well."

"That sounds complicated."

"Nah. It's very simple. I can show you if you want to monitor your wife. That is what I use to monitor my boyfriend."

"No need for that. Maybe to monitor my daughter because she seems to be growing wild. But even that will not be necessary. You see, man is not God. It is God who must know everything. Me I am fine with the little I know. I don't need to probe beyond the ordinary so I can keep my sanity."

"True talk. No be every rain drop dey fall for person roof… Last chance. Send me your account number."

"No, my dear. I won't be able to enjoy such money. Give it out to someone who needs it more."

"Alright sir if you insist. You are a very decent man sir. When I grow up I want to be like you," she said laughing. He too laughed heartily. "Sir I will keep in touch. When I am wedding, I will like you to be my godfather. In fact, I will like you to be my godfather going forward."

"No problem. I will introduce you to my wife. She will do a better job."

"What will you tell her sir, that I am the girl you tried to f*k without a condom?"

He laughed again heartily.

"So maybe we wait till your wedding then."

"No wahala sir. I will be in touch."

"Ciao."

She ended the call. They sat for a while in silence. It

was becoming dark and the lights were reflecting on the waters, the flashes of hundreds of headlamps that sped along the bridge above.

"So why did you do this?"

"Hack your phone? I wanted to prove something to him."

"I don't mean that. When you discovered what you saw, why didn't you go to him and make your hundred K?"

"My dear Big Sister. What would I achieve then? Possibly I ruin a happy home, make a happy and contented man inconsolable? For what? To prove the ancient truth that man is fallible? You know recently a girl sent a message to my boyfriend asking him to watch me that I am a *runs* girl. I had already seen the message she sent so I accused him of cheating on me and insisted to check his phone. He refused to give it to me. He said 'It's not every truth you must follow through.' And till date he has not mentioned the matter. I am doing it not because of you but because of your husband. When I met him I knew humanity still has hope. There are still decent people, and I don't want him to shatter that hope he has in others too. He lives his life as if the world is a good place, and indeed it is a good place for all that want to see the goodness in it. He sees you as perfect. And isn't that a good thing? I am sure your children too have grown up believing same; even if their experiences differ, what you have implanted in them would be the default."

Ono broke down and began to cry again uncontrollably. Yenny was surprised. Those who were strolling by turned and gave them a look. "Madam. You are calling attention to us," she said and gave her a tissue. She breathed in and out heavily and wiped off her tears.

"I am sorry. I have been such a disappointment. If not for this social media, I would have no such temptation nor dream of committing such acts…"

"Madam social media na media o," Yenny cut in. "It is only a tool. It sends out what you put in. If you put in good it sends good out and if you put in bad it sends it out. But the good and the bad is in ourselves."

Ono cried some more, realizing the truth that it is 'not what goes into a man that defiles him but what comes out of him.' She couldn't exonerate herself and blame social media. Even if it had become easier to forsake cherished values, it was because deep down, there was a tendency in each one to go against the norm, to be free without being responsible, to act without considering consequences.

"I am so unworthy of him," she said. "I promise myself I will not betray my husband's trust anymore. I promise myself. But please. He seems to like you by the way he laughs. You seem to put him at ease. You know how men are. Please promise me that you will stay away from him. Please. I beg you. Please."

"Madam. You see that your husband? I won't promise you that I will stay away from him o. I will make him my mentor. But be assured that even if he wants it, I will not open my legs for him. Who wan spoil I go hep am spoil but who no wan spoil I go hep am pure. And don't think I will use this anywhere against you. Me myself I am going to stop a lot of things. I don't want my boyfriend to find me out. I love him. I want him to marry me. I just need a good job. That Ekus ehn na wicked man. How him go dey f*k him friend wife like dat sef. I fit arrange sef make dem do im wife too."

"Are we back there again? Please let bygones be bygones."

"Okay na. Madam. You know say I fit get access to your devices. If I hear *pim* from you like this, dat one the whole world will hear o. I can't have you fooling a very decent man like dat. I go just arrange f*k am till im brains commot for head."

"Please now. Please. I won't do it again."

"My eyes are on you. Give me your account number make I return your money as e be say him no wan collect the bet prize."

"No na. Ehya. You are a decent girl after all. Don't worry. Keep it."

"Before nko? I be decent girl o. My own sef na *opendential* no be some people wey dey do like santa maria meanwhile dem dey f*k behind. Have a good evening," she said standing up.

"Which way are you going? I can drop you off."

"Don't worry. I will buy one or two things at the mall before I go home. I will do *taxify*."

As Ono walked away, she turned back and looked at Yenny who was still standing on the spot looking across the water under the reflection of light. Some people bring trouble into your life while some trouble your life to assume its authenticity. Somehow, she saw Yenny as the angel sent to trouble her life back on track, in her feisty and digital subtle ways. How old was she even? Maybe twenty three? Her daughter's age maybe and yet capable of so much. What was her own first daughter capable of? You only brought children into the world and did the best you could for them hoping the seeds you sowed would grow into something fruitful. She couldn't even imagine her daughter sleeping with any man. But it wasn't a matter written on the face. As Yenny had said, it wasn't every truth one must follow through but one thing she knew was that these devices in their hands, though capable of much goodness, were a *resurrector* of sorts, charming up 'the beast in us'; they were a coin with a very rough edge that crashed walls and boundaries, imprisoning restraint, redefining morals, mainstreaming deviance and ruining good men and women. True, even if their brand was not all Apple, they were all an apple herding Eves and Adams away from their innocence.

BOOK TWO

EBONY ANGEL

1.

How much was he really worth?

Liquid assets roughly amounting to about seven hundred and twenty million naira which if you converted to United States dollars amounted to just 2 million dollars! He considered himself poor even though he had three properties in Abuja, two in Lagos and five in his home state. He had only one property in London and was negotiating for another in Orlando Florida and by the time he paid for it his liquidity would shrink making him still poorer. The good thing was that he had just been elected the governor of his state. He had just concluded his asset declaration and the asset staff at the Code of Conduct Bureau (CCB) had advised him to escalate his assets. "Just project how much you might be worth at the end of your first term and indicate that in the declaration form," he was advised. The asset form was meant to be reviewed every four years.

So, he had written on the form that he was worth 8.5 billion naira in cash, a 50-room hotel and two commercial plazas. He knew that as governor with his security votes alone, he could save up to three billion naira a year not counting the returns that came from contracts awarded to cronies. Whatever the actual cost of a contract it was standard practice to put a 20% upscale amount which was remitted upfront before the contract began. The contractor would then use the 10% remaining from the initial mobilization sum and struggle to get the next stage of payments. Sometimes it took so long to get the second tranche and the contractor would abandon the contract. Some foolish contractors actually went to the bank to get loans to complete the contract having paid away the initial mobilization as upfront settlement for the contract, they would then spend years trying to get their money from government while the loan tenure expired and the interest mounted up, eating up whatever profit they would have made when they were paid eventually. The Nigerian government was the most effective agent of impoverishment! Well. That happened to fools, they ought to know that no one was to take government seriously. The wise guys were those who got the contracts, received the initial mobilization, made their upfront settlements, wrote reports for completion of first phase and made requests for second phase and vanished until payment for second phase was done. Indeed, this was how he had made most of his money. He was a specialist in cooking up fictitious projects and project reports, paying upfront from the mobilization, pocketing the balance and doing nothing more because no one was going to ask him any questions without answering some themselves. He was always sought out by those in government because he knew how to make things work for everyone without getting anyone in trouble especially when a government came that attempted to fight corruption.

As for the security vote, whoever thought of it was a genius. It was money no one expected you to account for. In his own state, it totaled to more than seven billion naira annually, and assuming he did some good security work with the money at all, there was no way he was not going to walk home with less than half the amount, and if he was a little prudent, he could walk home every year with up to five billion naira from the amount instead of three. And this is not counting other sources such as foreign travel allowances or *estacode* as they called it, money from the ecological fund, excess crude account, percentages from foreign loans etc. The prospect of making up to ten billion naira a year nearly blew his brains off. He took out his phone and calculated what it was worth in United States Dollars. If this was when the dollar was worth 200 naira this would be a staggering 50 million US dollars a year but now the dollar was worth 360 naira which meant he would be making approximately 27 million dollars a year. He multiplied that by four years and came up with about a hundred and eleven million dollars. He felt a little downcast because he hoped he could clock a minimum of 200 million US dollars in four years. He was sadder still when he remembered that he may have to keep a large chunk of money for his reelection. He was almost depressed when he remembered that those grand patrons who supported him during the elections would want a constant piece of the action. Then he brightened up a bit when he remembered that he had spare two billion naira from the security vote which could be so deployed. Indeed, settling these grand patrons was an utmost security initiative otherwise they had a way of making the soles of your shoes slippery. But one thing he would resist with all his tact would be to be a puppet governor. He wouldn't go through all this for some big man to press his remote button.

And what he loved most was the fact that as governor, he was above the law, because the law granted him immunity. He could even kill, annex people's properties, cancel licenses and deeds and go scot-free because as long as he was governor he could not be prosecuted whether for a crime or a civil matter. He could be investigated of course but that was only on paper because no one really did. Besides his party ruled at the center and as long as you were a party member the law looked at you lovingly. The truth was that there was really no opposition, all of them belonged to the same interests and who would now come and persecute a bird of the same flock when he or his cronies could be in the same situation too? It was only when Nigerians made a lot of noise on social media that government sometimes pursued grudgingly the prosecution of so-called looters. The fact was that to be a governor was difficult and having become one, it was one of the most rewarding offices on earth, materially. Good a thing the citizens too seemed to know that once you became governor the resources were for you to do as you pleased and were only good at writing funny criticisms on social media. He chuckled as he teased some critics in his heart; did they think Naija was United Kingdom or America where officials of government were stupid enough to resign at the flimsiest of scandals? How on earth did a government official resign because he arrived late or because he posted a nude picture to a girl which was intercepted! What did that have to do with being governor? Didn't a public official have a life? Here in

Naija even as a politician you slept with as many girls as you wanted and no one gave a damn about it. Is it when you had become governor, when citizens would even think that it was your entitlement that someone would make a case out of a man sleeping with a girl? How would a man make so much money and stick only to a wife he had been married for over fifteen years? 'What is money without a woman ?' he whispered to himself.

2.

As he thought about girls his mind flashed back to one he met in the state capital when he was part of an advance party to welcome Mr. President during a state visit. This was months before he relocated for the campaigns that led to his election as governor. His chauffeur took him to Crunches because he wanted to have a quick bite. Sometimes he just enjoyed being like every other person and going by himself into an eatery or lounge. Those who recognized him would give him a glance and smile. He had limited such interactions when the spate of kidnappings increased in the once peaceful state. But this day he couldn't restrain the urge of having a sit out by himself.

He had already finished his bite and was about leaving when he saw her. Youngish, with an almost shy innocent pleasant countenance, naturally complexioned as if a delicate brown polish had been applied all over her skin, a model's height with an appropriately endowed front and backside, she was the kind of girl who unintentionally caused a stir of stares once she walked into a place. She had this nose ring which made her appear such an easy take but then an aura that fenced her off as a snob. She seemed to realize that any make-up would hide her natural glow and wore none. She was in the company of another girl who was not bad but was nothing compared to that ebony angel. She probably had the self-awareness of her effects on people and so had a focused gaze, the way a celebrity knows she is recognized by everyone but minds her business. Only her friend threw a glance his way and smiled seeing the way he was looking at them. He cleared his bill, stood up and went to his car, deciding to sit and wait for whenever they would be leaving.

He walked with a slight limp. He had wrestled with polio as a child. He was just lucky that it was detected quite early and treated but it left him with a slightly smaller and shorter right leg. This he compensated for with his handsome features, fair skin, pointed nose and ears that just really fitted as if they were custom designed. He garnished all these with a sense of humour and a deep pocket. He had long come to know that the only ugly man was a poor man. At 51 he had already worked hard enough to get any woman he wanted. The only problem was that whenever he put on much weight, his limping became more obvious and sometimes he had to walk with a stick, which he incorporated as part of his swagger.

Apparently they came for a take away because not long afterwards he saw them coming out. His chauffeur honked and it was the friend that turned. The ebony angel kept moving without even a glance at his direction. He wound down the window slightly, enough for his hand to make a beckoning signal. Her friend responded. He found out that her friend's name was Cherry, got her number and said he would call her to meet that evening. She seemed excited. He could not wait for the evening and called her two hours later to come to his hotel. He could sense the excitement in her voice. "You can also come with your friend", he said very casually to her. He wanted the girl to think she was the one sought after. The girl called to inform him that another of her friends had joined them and they did not want to leave her behind. He told her he did not mind, she too could join in.

Time was not flying. He nearly called again but restrained himself. He mustn't sound so desperate. Finally, there they were. While the two girls dressed to kill, the ebony beauty was still dressed the same way, a pair of jeans and a Tee-shirt. She didn't even apply make-up. He greeted them cheerfully, offered them drinks and wasted no time inviting her into the bedroom. "See Cherry. I am sorry but it's your friend that I want. Can you ask her to come into the room ? Don't worry I will settle you properly."

"So its Nene you want…" Cherry left him with a frown on her face and went back to call her friend. She whispered to them that since she was on her period, the man needed someone who was not on her period and among the three of them Nene was the only one not on her period so could she go and talk to the man? Nene was upset. "What nonsense is that? So, he will see someone for the first time and just have sex with them?" Cherry begged her to just go in and listen to the man without admitting that she just made up the story to cover her embarrassment.

He could see that Nene was frowning. He could not guess what it was but he decided to take things easy. He introduced himself properly as someone contesting for the governorship of the state and that he had apologized to her friend and told her it was not she he wanted. "But you."

"And what makes you think I am interested?" That had unbalanced him a bit because girls in the capital city were always looking for men such as himself to be acquainted with. Besides her disposition didn't give her away as someone with such assertiveness.

"And why would you not be interested? Don't you know who I am?"

"Of course, I see you in the news but that doesn't mean I should jump at everything you say."

"You are proving hard to get right?"

"Me prove hard to get?" She actually hissed and stood up to walk away.

"Okay. Wait. I'm sorry. That didn't come out well."

"Apology accepted. Anyway Dr. Ekpes let's not beat about the bush. I know what men like you want. You see a girl, you sleep with her and move on to the next girl. Well, I refuse to be a sample."

"Sample?"

"Yes o. Is this not all it's about? Okay you give some money, and so what! What about my dignity that has been thrashed?"

"Wao. You are deep. It's long I met a girl like you."

"Don't flatter me please. How can you replace me with my friend just because she told you she is on her period? You think I am a commodity?"

"No, No. Now wait." He didn't like the way the girl was putting him on the defensive but at the same time he was really getting impressed. "I didn't say that to your friend but don't ask her. Believe me I got her number because of you and I invited her here because of you."

Nene was quiet for a moment. She believed him

because this would be the third time someone would be doing this, getting her friend's number so he could get to her. She wondered why those men thought her friends were the gatekeepers. She knew she had this self-contented, deceptively shy, vulnerable but snobbish look which made men almost unsure whether she would even talk to them.

"You were not looking my way and I didn't want to call much attention. But you are here now and I am here. I really like you. Let's be friends."

"I am not ice cream," she said laughing. "I know that tomorrow you will say the very same thing to another girl. And another. And another. I have since closed my mind to such stuff. Two of my friends are here. You can try any of them, although I must warn you that you will swim in rivers of blood."

"Rivers of blood?" He frowned confused.

"Their monthly period! Chei. See how fear catch you." And she laughed again. He laughed too, and a sort of connection was established between them, he with a certain respect towards her and she with a certain irreverence. It was at that point he swore that no matter how long it took he would sleep with her. He would keep her as one of his regulars, especially now that he had become governor, he would make sure she attended international conferences with him. No girl would refuse such a bait. He picked up her phone and quickly dialed his number with it so he could save it in his.

"What's the full name? And email address too." She told him. "I will get in touch with you."

"Please only get in touch for things that will build me up otherwise don't bother." She said.

"My dear don't you think you are overpricing

yourself? Remember that girls are available two for a penny o." He regretted it the moment he said it.

"Then buy them. Me am priceless." She stood up to leave. "How many men would one sleep with? Every day I am called aside by a man and all he wants is sex. I am so used to it I don't even give a thought to it. They have nothing to add to your life than to satisfy themselves. Don't even think that I will remember we met because tonight you will meet another and another will want to meet me tomorrow. It's a nuisance cycle."

"Hmmm. Serious girl. So okay if I say let's travel next month to Dubai, won't you come? Isn't that something?"

"Dr. Ekpes I won't tell anyone you said that because that comes out so cheap. So, your daughter walks up to you out of the blue and tells you I am going to Dubai and you allow her just like that. Would you be a good father? If you would, my dad would not, and even if he wouldn't know if I did, I would not embark because it ends up raising false expectations and a false lifestyle. Tomorrow you will take another girl to Dubai isn't it? Maybe my friends would be impressed. But I have been everywhere with dad and mum before mum died. So, go and impress someone else."

"Please wait. I see you want to be treated specially. I promise…"

She smiled. "Looks like I am not communicating well. Get in touch if you genuinely wish to help me grow. Otherwise don't bother. Have a good day sir." She reached for the door.

"Who told you I am done with you?" he said with a smile.

"You are sir. You have nothing new to say." She said

laughing. "Anyway. I am done. My dad would be needing me to serve his meal. He is diabetic."

"Oh, sorry about that. I hope he is receiving proper care."

"Yes sir. He is annoyingly careful and healthier than the healthy." And she laughed again.

"I see why you can't go very far away. We'll get him a nurse. Don't worry. Not even a hug?" he said and opened wide his arms. She smiled and stretched out her right hand, raising it up a bit.

"Be a gentleman and kiss my hand instead."

He held it for a brief moment, caressing it. He knew the gesture was actually supposed to be from a lady of equal or higher standing to a man but here he was about to kiss the hand of a kid. If he did so it meant she had put herself on an equal or higher pedestal. Maybe by her moral authority. Then he kissed it as she was about withdrawing her hand.

That was nearly a year ago and since then he had not stopped thinking of her; she had had such profound effect on him especially in the way it hadn't seemed to matter to her how wealthy he was or who or what he was. She would pick his calls and answer very politely and never respond to any suggestive messages he sent on WhatsApp until he tired out. Even when he became governor, apart from the congratulatory message she sent to him, she never sent any other messages. She never responded when he asked for her account number. She only said politely that when she was broke she would let him know. What was a better way of telling a rich man off? He had put her number on speed dial and prioritized her calls which never came. He planned to give her a place in his government. A young girl with such values could actually prove to be an asset and could be a major influence on the young. The problem was that when he met her she had only just finished school and had not gone on the compulsory national youth service. He was sure she was far into the service year now. Otherwise he would have to wait until she was done or reach out to the commandant to redeploy her to the state. She could serve out her position as part of national youth service and start earning the proper salary when the service year was over. But no matter how long it took, he would sleep with her. It was a vow.

He would burden her with so much trust and responsibility and make her so grateful that she would be the one to offer herself. He knew women well enough to know that they always wanted to offer something in return. He loved the fact that she was assertive and not afraid of him at all. He would use that to his advantage. She would be his conscience. He wondered how his own daughter fared, whether she ever had such exposure to men and how she would react in such circumstances. He found out later that Nene was the last daughter of the late Prof Nsima who was a gender activist. No wonder. He remembered Prof Nsima walking him out of her office five years ago over a favour he went to curry for his 'cousin.' It was about an exam she took for the second time and was going to be let off from the program without graduating. The woman had asked him if he had no shame. "This is academics not politics. Get out of my office." He could then understand the strong sense of values that Nene had. He might surprise everyone by naming her into his cabinet as a Special Adviser however young she appeared to be.

3.

He was heading to the airport.

 He was trying to get used to these protocols. He had to be in Abuja and protocol had chartered a private jet. He loved the paraphernalia and the opulence the office presented. For instance, about forty cars were in his convoy to the airport with expert outriders and sirens. He wanted to ensure that it got established in the minds of people, especially his opponents, that there was a governor in town. It was easy to know when he was in town because everywhere he went, there was a long convoy blocking traffic. He did not really care how people felt about it, they should know that the Governor was passing by and should find another route, especially these people in the city, as majority of them did not actually vote for him, if not for the insight he had and prepared in advance.

You see elections in Nigeria is by voting and fine tuning. Some people call it rigging but it was simply fine tuning the process for a true winner because you couldn't leave that choice entirely to the people who sometimes didn't know their left from their right. As soon as the national chairman of the party had been elected, he Ekpes went to him on a courtesy visit and brought him two hundred thousand dollars. He had simply gone to the bureau de change and converted the naira equivalent to the US dollar because big men in Nigeria did not receive naira as gifts but foreign currency. By that act he established himself as having interest in the office. He pledged his loyalty to him and promised that should he win the nomination and election subsequently he would put him on a monthly security allowance. He didn't state the amount though. He practically knelt down before the party chairman to tell him he entirely depended on him to see that he got nominated. One way was for him to agree that he make input into the persons sent to the state to conduct the party primaries. He was able to get a heads up before even the appointees knew they were the returning officers for his state primaries.

He visited each of them separately and introduced himself as an aspirant and flattered each one by telling them to exert their influence on the party leaders so that he would be considered the party's candidate in the state. He didn't tell them he had even suggested their names for nomination. He gave the five of them ten thousand dollars each without each one knowing he had met the other. Luckily, three of the five were chosen to come to his state as returning officers. As soon as he learnt of this he reached out to them separately and made promises, with the gift of an additional cash of twenty thousand US dollars each. As for the actual primaries, he had lobbied the state party executive to have an open primary not a delegate election. This was because it was more difficult to take care of delegates. Delegates made sure they collected money from every candidate and then voted for the highest bidder. He did not know how much his opponents would give but he thought that it was more participatory for party members to have a voice so he had taken good care of the state party chairman who insisted primary elections take place at chapter level and collated by the state Exco. He made sure he visited every ward in the state and listened to their expectations and then took good care of the ward Exco and similarly the chapter Exco. At the last count he had spent over a hundred million naira in this process.

He got his IT assistant who regularly sent the ward Exco bulk short messages, which acted as a bulletin about his initiatives. He made them feel carried along and dependable. He told them they could contact him by sending text messages if any ward member had a personal issue to resolve so he kept aside about ten million naira for emergency family needs. Of course, not long afterwards the dedicated number was bombarded with pleas for school fees, medical bills, rent, farm preparation and so on. Since he had advised that an account number be accompanied, his assistant would transfer an amount to the recipient. Soon even without winning the nomination, he had established a reputation as a compassionate person. Strangely, he actually enjoyed this aspect of reaching out to the people in this manner and didn't mind that within six months he had spent over sixty million naira. He never refused anyone no matter how foolish the request appeared to be, he might drastically reduce the amount but no one was rejected; the person only had to be a party member because he had insisted that anyone making a request must identify himself with his membership number. Other candidates accused him of campaigning beforehand but there was really no evidence because his bulk text messages and WhatsApp groups only talked about his humanitarian initiatives and getting the right candidate for every office without mentioning his name. Anyway no one took him to court over the matter. His nomination became a very smooth issue.

He applied the same strategy with the National Electoral Commission (NEC). NEC was organized in a pyramidal manner; there was a national commission made up of a commissioner from each of the six geopolitical zones, headed by a chairman. The chairman was usually the CEO of NEC and the returning officer for the presidential elections. The commission was fed by a resident commissioner in each state known mostly as RC. The RC had a team of directors in charge of various sectors. At the local government level, there was the Local Government Electoral Officer or LEC as they were called. To win in an election, your party had to be familiar with these LECs because the actual election took place at local level. And then you had to know the RC as well because with instructions from above no matter how strong you were on ground, things could change. Sometimes you were lucky to have a stubborn RC who would insist on returning those the results showed had won. The RC was the returning officer for national assembly and gubernatorial elections while the LEC was responsible for the state house of assembly elections. He had long before the elections met all of the 18 LECs and settled them. Even if they were to be swapped for electoral duties, he had been able to meet with each of them and they would know what to do, except they wanted to work for the highest bidder. Politics in Naija was cumbersome. The sheer man hours put into meeting and settling officials was something else.

Surprisingly the actual elections were simple. Because his party won at the national level, the electorate felt it was better to align with the national government rather than be ostracized. He received more votes than he expected. Luckily the turn out wasn't massive so his party agents and the opposition party agents whom he had settled in advance, assisted in boosting the votes by voting on behalf of those who had not turned out for the election. The votes went his way and he was declared governor. Elections in Nigeria were a combination of money and more money, access to officials, and ability to secure post-voting votes.

"And after you have gone through all this, one arm chair civil society critic would come and start writing nonsense!" he murmured under his breath. He decided there and then that he would brook no opposition. The route to this office was treacherous and only for the brave. He would govern the way he deemed fit and anyone who did not like it could try to become governor or relocate to another state.

4.

He gazed through the window as the plane took off. It was a Gulfstream G550 business jet made by Gulfstream Aerospace, a subsidiary of General Dynamics in Savannah, Georgia US. It could fly a range of twelve thousand five hundred and one kilometers at a top speed of 941 km per hour and had a wing span of 28 meters. He had tried to make enquiries about the cost of a new one and he found out it cost not less than forty-two million dollars. He would still find a way of getting a used one because it was becoming a status symbol to own a private jet. He might perhaps buy it with state funds and then alienate it to himself or a crony after his second term as governor. It was so luxurious up here, the white leather seats, the mahogany tables; this one even had a bedroom in case one wanted to sleep. He had never had sex up in the sky, maybe he would try someday.

He looked out again. He could see the shiny new roofs and the old rusty zinc roofs as they all faded from view. It struck him that somehow that was how life was, both the old and new would fade one day. If those roofs could speak they would tell stories of the different take offs and landings of presidents and royalties and VIPs. And governors as they rushed to Abuja for one meeting or other, as you couldn't really do anything without Abuja! In Nigeria you had to incentivize for everything to be done. If you stayed back in the state they would think you were not serious and would grant approvals for other states and leave yours behind even for things that were statutory.

As usual, ten of his aides had accompanied him on this trip including security. He could not understand what all of them were coming to do and this was sounding so invasive into his space but then there was nothing he could do because he was told it was the protocol. He had no more privacy. This was why people brought those they could absolutely trust, as aides. He was sure it would be in the news that afternoon and in the night that he was out of state. Now he was the news, everything he did was news worthy.

He counted himself lucky that he was not a governor in America or Europe where even though everyone had a choice to live the way they wished, they still held their public officials to the highest moral standards. What hypocrisy!

They had reached their cruising altitude and the pilot had announced that in five minutes they would begin a gradual descent into Nnamdi Azikiwe International Airport Abuja. He settled down to be ready for the descent. He had come to know that taking off and landing were the dangerous moments for an aircraft. When a plane was at cruising level hardly did one have anything to fear unless there was a mechanical or electrical fault or except they met extremely bad weather. He remembered the return leg trip he made to the UK recently through Frankfurt and how as the plane began taxing for takeoff a baby was crying uncontrollably. A doctor examined the baby and confirmed it sick so the parents had to disembark. As soon as they turned to leave the aircraft, the baby stopped crying. Because their luggage had to be disembarked the passengers had to wait for an hour or so. It was when they were set to continue with the journey that it was discovered there was an electrical fault. They spent another two hours trying to fix it but to no avail so they had to transfer them to another aircraft after spending more than five hours waiting. Whenever he thought of the incident, he knew that God had used the crying baby to save them because the fault would have been discovered midair. Life was really a mystery. Babies were angels even if they could only talk by crying.

He always looked forward to the announcement of reaching the cruising altitude and preparation for descent. It was always reassuring.

5.

Suddenly there was a very sharp drop and the plane began to make a free fall. Everyone without exception began screaming and praying. His heart beat so fast it could be heard above the vibration. The air hostess who had been standing, stumbled and hit her shoulder on the seat just as the captain's voice sounded that everyone should have their seatbelts on as they had a situation which he would bring under control. The plane had fallen through a thick cloud and was shoved everywhere for a very long minute. He closed his eyes and began to whisper "God help me. God help me." He made all kinds of pledges, the way a man begged for his life before someone who was holding a gun and ready to pull the trigger. His entire life came to him in a flash and he realized that he was not ready. If he died now his family would be in a shambles because he had not made a will, and most painfully, his deputy would take over when he had not enjoyed being governor for even a full one month. He would head straight to hell. What kind of hard luck was this! 'God why? Why me?' he began to cry softly as his aides were not making any pretensions about their plight and were wailing and praying loudly, casting and binding. 'God why me? Others become governors and govern for eight years and retire to the senate and in my own case I have only been a governor for twenty-four days! God please have mercy on me and I promise to serve your people with all my heart if you give me this one chance. Please God do not disgrace me. Please have mercy on me. I will start going to church every day please Lord. Have mercy on me... Every Sunday I mean. Lord please have mercy on me.'

The turbulence continued for several minutes.

All he had and all his plans seemed not to matter anymore. All he wanted at this very critical moment was just to be alive. 'What a gift life is,' he thought. And yet he had been blind to it, seeking to acquire and amass without a thought it would one day come to nothing if he dropped dead. Like now. It dawned on him why people like him were afraid to die.

His eyes were still closed. He could not look. Maybe something had malfunctioned and the controls were no more working because the aircraft kept being tossed up and down and vibrating violently. A moment later the pilot's voice came on. He apologized for the situation and said the aircraft would soon stabilize and that they would be climbing a higher altitude shortly before descending again. He explained that they had just avoided a head on collision with another aircraft. 'What! Head on collision! Were they on the highway or up in the sky ? Jeez! How come there could be a head on collision in midair, did the radar fail to notify the oncoming aircraft? 'My goodness!' He said to himself, wagging his head. 'Wonders shall never end.' He counselled himself that he had to appear strong because he was being looked upon as a leader. Someone had said that being courageous didn't mean one wasn't afraid but to make sure the fear did not show and the fear did not stop what had to be done.

True to the pilot's words, the aircraft stabilized and began to make a slight ascent. The pilot announced that he had been warned that there was a very rare strong westerly wind blowing across but that they would be fine as he would do his best to land or divert to a nearby airport if he could not land. And that was how he went into panic mode again.

Everywhere went absolutely quiet, with everyone praying in their hearts for a safe landing. It struck him again how vulnerable the most powerful of men were and yet behaved as if they were immortal. Long ago at a funeral service for his friend's son who was a pilot, the priest had advised that each time one needed to board a plane they should do so as if it was their last journey and should see every safe landing as a fresh opportunity given by God for a better life. He hadn't given much thought to that advisement because he knew that aircrafts were the safest means of transportation. Now he could hear Fr. Itanja talking again.

If indeed he landed safely, then it was a fresh start for him. Somehow, he felt an inner assurance that he would survive today because a few days ago he had dreamt and seen himself in Abuja meeting with the president. Even though he had stopped being prayerful he still had a sense of the immediate future through his dreams. He believed the dream was a postdated indication that he would be in Abuja no matter what. He promised himself that if he survived this situation, he would do his best under the circumstances to be a different man.

"Please prepare for landing," the captain said and assured them again that it will be alright. He resumed his prayers. He must look for his rosary, now he was counting his fingers and praying the Hail Marys, mixing up the words. He would really need to go back and practice his faith again. He had received a letter from the Catholic Bishop inviting him to a meeting in his office and he had not replied yet. He did not want to give the impression that he was partisan; as governor he didn't want to be seen as belonging to any particular church or faith. But now he promised he would go looking for the Bishop and accept the offer of a chaplain to government house.

They could now see the city. The plane was unsteady as the wind appeared to be very strong. It appeared to be raining heavily. They attempted to land but were swept off by a strong wind. For a moment he thought they were going to crash as the plane fluttered but the pilot appeared to be an excellent one as he maneuvered the plane and ascended again. He circled around for a while and made three different attempts to land and failed. He then announced that if they did not succeed with the fourth attempt he would go and land in Kaduna and wait for the weather to clear. As he opened his eyes for a moment and looked out, he could see at a distance that fire trucks were at alert. He took out his phone to call his wife as they circled around for a longer while. He knew it was against aviation protocol but he wanted to tell her he loved her. He did not remember the last time he said that to his wife. His wife did not pick. He switched off the phone again and shook his head. How often he took for granted the opportunities that appeared so insignificant but which were the daily epochs of life. If God would save him this once he would tell everyone he needed to say so that he loved them. He wouldn't wait until when he was afraid to die.

The thought of death frightened him again. How did the other side really look like? Was he ready for it? What if they crashed during this fourth attempt and he did not survive or became invalid like one of his colleagues who survived a plane crash only to lose all memory and motor abilities? He began to pray again from the depths of his heart.

Then they made their last attempt. They had been hovering for nearly two hours; though the plane was fluttering like a bird against a strong wind, it pushed ahead resolutely and touched the ground and then embarked on a high speed and shortly afterwards the speed breakers spread out and it began to slow down but not without skidding off the runway onto the grass before it came to a final stop. His aides broke into song *"We are saying thank you Jesus, Thank you my Lord. We are saying Thank you Jesus, Thank you my Lord…"* The pilot walked over and explained to them that were this aircraft not to be a sophisticated one, they would have collided midair but that the aircraft had ACAS, an airborne collision avoidance system that functioned independently of ground based equipment and air traffic control, that the sharp drop was the maneuver initiated automatically by the system to avoid metal to metal collision but unfortunately they had descended into a region of very bad clouds and had also met a wild wind. He explained that the wind rarely occurred but that aircrafts were always equipped to handle such occurrences, that it was his first time of encountering that kind of wind on landing.

"But I thought aircrafts had regulations about flying separate paths," the governor asked.

"Yes Sir. That is the ASAS, the airborne separation assurance system. The next aircraft is supposed to be 5 nautical miles in the horizon, or about 300 meters vertically. I don't really know what happened in this case but our plane was equal to the task. I am sure traffic control will tell us."

"Five nautical miles…"

"That's like 9.3 kilometers sir."

"Anyway Captain. Thanks a lot. You saved our lives today. God used you to save us. I owe you," he said, giving him his card. "Send me an SMS with your full name within the hour on your mobile please."

"Thank you, sir. I will. Actually, the weather was even more of a challenge sir. But I am glad we made it to the ground."

I am glad we made it to the ground. It was truly something to be thankful for, to make it to the ground, alive. He wagged his head in true appreciation of the predicament he had just survived. The fire service trucks were already on ground and they had to disembark in an emergency protocol. They could carry their bags though since there really was no fear of the plane bursting into flames. The airport authorities came with a van and picked them all to the VIP lounge while their luggage would be sorted. He understood they would have to tow the plane to a hangar. Meanwhile all flights had been suspended from landing or taking off because of the mishap.

<h2 style="text-align:center">6.</h2>

He received a call from Mr. President who asked how he was, that he was informed about his plight though he learnt everything was under control. He thanked Mr. President sincerely for reaching out. His phone kept buzzing. His PA kept answering certain calls on his behalf. His wife called and was weeping with joy. Then he saw a text message from Nene. "Sir I traveled today and just saw on social media that you escaped death. God be praised. There is a reason you are not yet dead. Thank God for life Sir."

Not yet dead ?

For a moment he pondered on what such a message could mean, as if he was destined to die and did not die yet, as if it was something he had escaped momentarily but which would surely come his way? Why didn't she say *There is a reason you did not die?* Why *not yet dead?* Was she wishing him dead? Perhaps he had allowed himself to be taken in too much by this girl. He would cease all communication with her. He would really have felt worse if not that he counseled himself with the truth that it was actually a fact that sooner or later he would die like every man on the face of the earth. He would block her number. Then he saw the adjoining text message *'Discover your purpose..'* He now understood better. Though he did not open it, he realized she was using a phone with a low memory and the SMS could not deliver all at once. He breathed a sigh of relief and put her back to her position in his heart. True. He didn't need to discover any more purposes. He already had a purpose. He was by the grace of God the executive governor of his state. The lesson he learnt today was that instead of seeing his state as a fiefdom or instead of seeing himself as emperor he was going to work his heart out to uplift his people.

He knew there were many constraints with regard to how the federation was structured but he wouldn't use that as an excuse; he was going to make government work for his people. Government wasn't the state, the state included many other actors in the civil society, including government. The mistake he had seen in the past was that his predecessors equated the state with government and made it seem as if an offence against the government was an offence against the state. The resources of the state were for everyone and not for the government to use as it pleased. He was going to open himself up to accountability and anyone who didn't want to work that way would have to find his way out.

His heart began to pump some adrenalin as he began to be purged of his self-centeredness. His country would have been a developed nation by now but for governors and presidents who thought only of the next election and life after office. Everything was structured to the advantage of the incumbent not the people he was to serve. But now a fire burned inside him. He had traveled round a lot and he had seen what small African countries were doing. If need be he would send civil servants down to those countries to understudy and develop some standard operating procedures for those initiatives back home. He would work hard first using all the resources available before asking people to pay more taxes. He would do his best to expand the tax base before even increasing taxes. He would consolidate all the taxes and stop hooligans chasing poor citizens about in the name of paying taxes. He would never fall into the stupid idea of abandoning roads just because they were federal roads, he would make sure he rehabilitated them and then pass the bill to the federal government to pay whenever they pleased. Roads he would love to repair in particular were roads leading to the border with other states and with Cameroun as this could open up international trade. He would take special interest in ensuring there was regional trade between the countries that were contiguous: Cameroon, Equatorial Guinea, Central African Republic. He would support concessions for a regional airline from his state capital to these countries because he had seen that the geographical distance between his state capital and the capitals of these countries was shorter than flying to Lagos or Abuja. These plans filled his head as he was being driven to Transcorp Hotel. His convoy in Abuja here had up to fifteen vehicles. One immediate thing he was going to do was cut down on these unnecessary expenditures. What did he need fifteen vehicles in Abuja for? That meant petrol for fifteen vehicles, salaries for fifteen drivers, inflated invoices for maintenance for fifteen vehicles etc. He would keep a liaison officer here in Abuja who would act as Special Assistant on many other things instead of bringing all these aides from the state.

He called the protocol officer.

"Cancel my reservation at Transcorp. I will go to my house and stay." He felt he had a duty to save the state's money whenever he could because a lot of money got wasted in such frivolities that there was no money really to do something substantial. As for his security vote, security was more than the absence of the risk to life; there was food security for instance, health security, financial security. He would use the funds to promote all these aspects of security.

"Sir what of the conference material?" *Conference material* were the girls they had arranged for him. He was to spend three nights, each night with two different girls.

"Cancelled too." Such things were far from his mind after surviving such an ordeal. He felt ashamed. "In fact, take me to a Catholic Church. I need to visit the chapel."

When he attended mass regularly early in his career, back in his capital city, the priest would encourage people to visit the chapel for quiet prayer. That was Fr. Itanja who was always filled with humour and would remind you that "My name is Ja for short," so they would call him Fr. Ja. The last time he heard of him he was heading an NGO owned by the church. He would say that there was no one way to pray, that even if you had nothing to say just go and report yourself to God and say 'Lord here I am, a sinner. I have come again. And then wait to hear from him...He will speak through your heart.' But he had never really paid attention to it. He knew his wife was doing all the praying on his behalf.

"Take me to the one in Area 3."

He had not been to church for more than a year. Since he moved to the nation's capital he would attend the evening masses on Sunday if at all. People hardly knew who he was in the parish because he was not part of any group in the church. He was always afraid of being known in the church because of undue demands on time and resources. He didn't understand why the priests spent so much time talking about money. That was why he started going to evening mass on Sundays in the first place and stopped altogether when they brought the same attitude to the evening mass. If they would only say what the need was and drop an account number for people to make contributions, it would work better for his kind of person than all the nuisance fund- raising every Sunday in church.

They got to the Church premises. He had requested that the siren not be blown but he was sure to still call attention by the number of cars that followed him so he asked that they close for the day except for his own vehicle and the security car. The gate opened for them immediately they realized it was a high government official. He asked where the chapel was and one of the church security officers offered to take him there. He came down from the vehicle and walked with the young man while the driver went to park the vehicle. His ADC was trailing behind him. The Protocol officer was supposed to give each of the *Conference Material* five hundred dollars; he had already collected the money from him, deciding that he would hand it over to any priest he saw within the premises.

"Excellency Sir you are my governor," the young man was saying.

"Really? You are from our state?"

"Yes sir. I learnt you nearly died today sir. God bless and keep you. You shall not die. You shall serve out your two terms in Jesus name. Amen."

"Amen. Thank you, my brother. Na God o. That is why I have come to thank him." He saw people whispering and looking his way, obviously in recognition of who he might be. "Why are you just a security man in the church?" he asked him.

"We all have dreams sir but sometimes they get scuttled. I took a year off to work and raise my fees in the university as I had no one to support me." Talk of scuttling... His would have been scuttled today.

"What were you studying?"

"Anatomy sir. That is the chapel sir. God bless you sir."

"Thank you very much my dear." As he made to go into the chapel he stopped and called the young man back. He gave him the envelope containing the three thousand dollars. "Use this for your education. Please don't waste it on any frivolous things. God bless you too." He felt that at that point the young man might be able to make use of the money better than if he saw a priest and just handed him the money. Priests did a lot of good and it was good to give them money but since this was a direct encounter, it wasn't necessary for any intermediation. If people could only regularly enquire about others, they would see opportunities to share in their lives.

7.

He saw that people took off their shoes. There were roughly nine wooden pews meaning it could seat roughly forty-five persons at a time but there were about six persons in the well finished and furnished room. He could vaguely notice a young lady at the far end corner with a travel bag praying. Maybe she was stranded. No loud prayers were aloud here. He went and sat in a corner.

He did not know when he dozed off. He only heard himself snoring away and woke with a start, embarrassed. It was already 7.15 pm and he had been there for about twelve minutes most of the time napping. He hoped he wasn't the one that drove people away because only the girl in the other corner was left. He couldn't really concentrate in any prayer. He had only said 'Thank you Lord for saving me. I am sure you did this for a purpose. Use me…"

Then it struck him that this was also a call, a vocation. Sometimes in church they talked about vocation to the priesthood, to married life, why didn't they talk about politics as a vocation? As governor it dawned on him that his call was as servant of the common good. It was a unique thing, to be chosen among nearly four million citizens to be the leader. He remembered how in school and fresh from university he had all kinds of ideas about an African renaissance. The civilization that built the pyramids wasn't Arab, it was the Nubians, black men. They invented the hieroglyphics and all those advances in civilization. His own ancestors in Ejagham land invented the *Nsibidi* form of writing. But now the black race was the butt of all other races, especially his country, so blessed and yet the poverty capital of the world. The constitution that existed, with the immunity given to them as governors encouraged them to see the state as their patrimony. There was no real sense of the common good because no one could hold them to account. How did you give so much powers to a human being and then expect him to be accountable? He resolved as he sat there before the Blessed Sacrament which Catholics believe is the real presence of Jesus Christ, that he Dr. Ekpes Akpeyange, he would serve as steward. The priest had explained one day that a steward was like head of a household who was given the latitude to manage the resources of the house the way he deemed fit on condition that he rendered account. A steward was almost like the owner, except that he had to render accounts to the real owner. The real owners of the state were not those grand-patrons, the real owners were every citizen of the state. He had to serve them, that was why he was a public servant. But what had he and his peers become ? Public Lords, Public Emperors...

Quickly he ran through the steps he would need to take. On his own he would go over the indicators of the Sustainable Development agenda and understand clearly how they could be domesticated in his circumstances because though acting locally he would love to see himself as contributing to global advancement.

He would convoke a citizens' assembly. He would ask for each constituency to choose two very educated persons, a man and a woman for the assembly. They would convene for three days. No hotels or per diem just lunch. No transport even. They should realize it was a new government. He would get someone from the NGOs to facilitate the assembly. They would together analyze the strengths, the weaknesses, the opportunities and threats to the state. He had seen documents carrying these things but he needed to have a fresh start. Besides what he saw was over ten years old. He would want the assembly to have input into a strategic direction for the state. From these participants, he might likely choose his team.

One other significant thing he was going to do was send an executive bill to the House of Assembly to kill the Local Government Joint Account law. It was a law his predecessors used in exploiting the local government system, taking away their allocations from the federation account and their autonomy. The law he was proposing would take things back to how they were long ago. He would ensure that while allocations came monthly from the federal government, the law would enable them to pass the allocations directly to the local governments. He would ensure free and fair elections were conducted into the local councils, as his predecessor had not allowed elections into the councils for years. This would reduce pressure on the state and ensure that citizens became more active politically at the local level. He would make the eligibility criteria for local government councils so high that only credible persons would go in there. Only people with a currently paying job or business complete with proper personal income tax receipts would make it.

On second thoughts he could experiment with consolidating all revenue, ensuring all local governments developed work plans for the year complete with a budget and they would draw down from the budget to implement. His commissioners would then be more or less as officers with MEAL capacities - Monitoring, Evaluation Accountability and Learning. Many years ago he had worked in an NGO before going into business, he would have to go back to that constituency because there was a lot of capacity there to move things ahead.

He would set up an anti-corruption agency, modeling it after the federal but in his own case, it would be more of application of technology to prevent corruption and because he himself would hold himself highly accountable he would deal mercilessly with those who thought it was business as usual. By the time he set example with his associates, everyone would sit up. From his days in the NGO he knew that if internal controls were very tight, corruption was reduced to a minimum and he knew of technologies that could tighten leakages. The treasury single account his predecessor had introduced made sure all incomes of the state went into a single treasury account, a good way to consolidate revenue and use it for the common good. Two areas he would invest in would be education and health. He would engage NGOs at local level to undertake registration of rural dwellers into a community health insurance scheme and deploy mobile clinics mostly in rural areas since it had been observed that rural dwellers hardly went to hospital. He would revive the essential drugs program and make drugs available free to those who had chronic conditions, akin to what the United States did with anti-retroviral therapy through PEPFAR. He would pay unscheduled visits to health centers, cottage hospitals in rural areas so that staff posted to local areas would take their duties seriously. He would set up a fund for serious ailments such as cancer, diabetes, complicated surgeries, and have a prenegotiated fee to settle the specialists in case of surgeries. He would apply nationwide for science teachers or abroad for volunteer science teachers for the rural schools since many indigenous teachers didn't love to stay in the rural areas otherwise he would introduce a special rural incentive including staff accommodation. He would liaise with the NGOs for special poverty programs and bring any corrupt NGO staff to book through monitoring. Government could not be at the forefront of everything when there were competent NGOs to handle these things on behalf of the state. Then he would ensure there was a list-serve that included all the churches and mosques in the state as part of the wider information outreach to citizens. He would work in close concert with the faith-based institutions with regard to their areas of expertise, especially education, health and poverty eradication and sub-grant to them to do these things on behalf of the state, after all their institutions were for the good of the citizens.

He would love to engage in mass social housing, in conjunction with the World Bank, which would translate into home ownership. For instance, he would discuss with property owners by the beach, resettle them with homes elsewhere, demolish the entire set of buildings in the area that were an eyesore and build high rises in the environment to accommodate more people. He would establish a fund for rural housing initiatives.

He would prevail on the local governments to register farmers and give stipends during the farming season while training youths on simple technologies of food preservation. There would have to be a task force on hinterland food evacuation during harvest time and incentives given to those wanting to invest in the value chains of the local farm produce especially in terms of food processing and storage.

As tourism was one of the main strengths of the state, he would ensure the concept of Rest House was resurrected. He grew up seeing rest houses built by the colonial masters in far flung locations, where they camped during tour duties. He would make sure there were rest houses built in locations with tourism potential and train community members to manage them.

One area in which he would take quite seriously was procurement. Procurement was the blood of corruption in government. He had been a contractor and knew all those tricks, so he would take it as a special area of monitoring. He would ensure contractors were promptly mobilized and fully paid on completion of jobs. Once he started to make things work there would be a rise in confidence in government ability to deliver. He would also focus on the civil service and retrain it towards a knowledge economy. He would negotiate with the unions in advance to insert a clause that promoted ease of doing business and appropriate penalties for civil servants who constituted a stumbling block to transactions. He would empower the state public complaints commission and make sure complaints were investigated and dealt with.

To raise money for all these things, he would reform the budget process. The budget was easily the greatest instrument of corruption. He would adopt the NGO model that ensured items were budgeted at unit cost, partnering with civil society organizations for budget monitoring.

Within this short period he had discovered that government incurred huge wastes just to run. He would have to go visit Peter Obi a former governor of Anambra State on how he cut the costs of governance. He knew that all these things were a tall order and he alone would not be able to accomplish them which was why he was in the right place to seek help. There would be many battles to fight as those who were bent on turning the state into a personal estate would fight dirty; they may even bribe the state legislature to impeach him. But he was sure that if his intentions were right, God would see him through and make him win the war on behalf of the people. He wanted people from his state to be proud. He would show that it was possible for things to work in Nigeria and gradually through his example, many other governors would sit up and do what was best for the people even if they couldn't avoid amassing state resources for themselves.

The truth was that it was so easy to please the average Nigerian. Sometimes all a Nigerian required from government was a good road because he could fetch his own water, produce his own electricity and find a way to educate his children but he could not construct a public road! He would definitely make sure the highways leading to the northern part of the state, the roads into the hinterlands of the rain forest communities, the roads to the boundaries with other states and other countries, were kept in good condition always no matter what it cost. He would leave a legacy in which government works and serves the people, while creating enabling environment for businesses to thrive, both small and big, with a strong civil society sector.

Civil society engagement was a goldmine for good governance and he wondered why his predecessors had not uncovered it. The way they worked then in NGO, they spent a long time planning and bringing out measurable indicators and outcomes. He may have to spend the first year mostly planning and then use the last three years executing the strategy. He would not take it for granted that he was entitled to eight years, because really what he was voted in for was a period of four years. He would so perform that it would be the people begging him for a second term. He would make the local government elections so transparent that credible persons would be attracted to contest for positions and therefore make his work easier. By the time all the local government areas were functioning, and those who were not efficient were dealt with severely, good governance would spread around like mushrooms. Towards the end of his tenure, after compiling enough data of the unemployed poor, he might toy with the idea of a universal basic income. He had read about states like California experimenting on it, he would study it more in his own context and apply it. The truth was that if he as the governor was committed and had a sense of the common good, a lot of wastage could be avoided which would free up funds for such social safety nets. If citizens saw the way the institutions were accountable, they would reduce the desire to manipulate them. He would support law enforcement to work and if they did not serve the state's purposes because the police is a federal agency, he would have his own vigilante groups and train them for crime control.

8.

By the time he checked his watch, it was a little over 8pm and he had read that the chapel closed by 8pm. He stood up with a start, said a brief prayer, genuflected and left the chapel. He could hear some singing at a distance. He had left his phone with his personal assistant who ran to him with it as soon as he saw him coming out. "Sir the vice president called and I told him you were praying in the church. Would you want to call him back now?"

He took the phone and dialed the VP's number. His personal assistant answered and said VP was in a meeting and that he would call back. For some reason he dialed Nene's number. It rang out the first time. Over time he had come to understand that you should call a lady at least twice, because their phones could be right inside the bag and by the time she managed to discover it the call would ring out. Then he called again and someone said behind him. "I am here Sir."

He had never been so startled. "What! Nene. It's you ! What are you doing here ? You traced me here ?" he said, as he turned around in bewilderment.

"No, your Excellency. I didn't even know you were here. I mentioned in my text message that I traveled. I arrived Abuja some hours ago and my sister happens to be a chorister so I had to come here to get the keys from her but she wanted me to wait for her that they would be done by 8.30. I decided to come to the chapel instead. I was here praying when I heard a man snoring. I was so astonished to see that it was you when I turned to look. I continued with my prayer when I saw you were in deep meditation but I have since been through and was waiting for when you would step out so I could come greet you so I thought you had seen me that was why you called. I came in from Ondo where I am serving, to spend some time with my sister. I have two weeks off before my POP and I don't want to go to the state."

"Wow. Wonders shall never end. What a coincidence. What is POP ? Plaster of Paris I guess?" he said laughing. "Oh yes Passing-Out-Parade for corps members. Congratulations. It means you would soon finish and be looking for a job."

"Why will I look for a job when a whole governor is my friend."

"So now you are happy to have a governor as your friend abi?"

"Yes now. Who no go happy?"

The governor's aide knew there must be something special between his boss and this young lady for her to be so assertive before him. He had never seen his boss become almost like a boy before any girl, the way he would tell him "Let me know when Nene calls…" although she hardly called, and sometimes he felt it was a coded way of asking him to tell Nene to call him but he had never met her until now and never knew how she would take it if he tried to give her the heads up.

"Actually, if there is anyone I needed to see right now, it's you. You either come with me gently or the security men would arrest you for breaching protocol," he said laughing.

"I hope you have your handcuffs," she said laughing. "Okay sir. I need to let my sister know. Can she come with me?"

"On second thoughts. Does she have her own place? Let me visit her instead. Would she have food in the house? I planned to stay in a hotel but I am no longer doing that. I am hungry."

"Excellency let me go and get her. I am sure she will be most pleased to serve you. I know she cooked plenty today because I was coming." And as if she was reading his mind. "She is single Excellency."

The way she rushed into the choir hall made everyone turn to look at her. Her sister stood up immediately thinking something was amiss. The singing was suspended for a moment. She didn't know when she blurted out. "Nene what is the problem?" and because everyone had a concerned look on their faces and she felt obliged to calm the tension Nene didn't even know when she blurted out "The governor wants to come to the house. He is hungry."

There was suppressed laughter and then a bit of murmuring which the choirmaster controlled. Many choristers wanted to excuse themselves to go out perhaps to witness the scenario of this hungry governor and wondered at the kind of relationship their member had with a governor that he would come crying for food in her house but the choir master did not allow them.

Quickly her sister packed her file and excused herself. She behaved as if it was one of those happenstances but her heart enlarged with elation. Her colleagues would be eyeing her with a certain deference and before long would be sending their CVs for jobs. Nene had told her the man had asked her out and still kept in touch but she didn't understand it was up to this level. The man must really like her sister to follow her here like this. Or maybe Nene came to Abuja because the man was coming? Thank God she lived in a good area, not far from the church actually, and thank God she had made two good pots of soup, *Afang* and *Banga,* enough to feed twenty persons. It would be a very great honour for her to entertain the governor in her house.

"Excellency, my sister Eka. Eka His Excellency Dr. Ekpes."

"Can you feed ten men?" was his greeting and laughter. She liked him immediately.

"With all pleasure sir. Pleased to meet your Excellency."

"Same here. I hope the road to your house is motorable," he joked.

"If it's not Sir, I am sure you will speak with the FCT minister, the mayor. Let me take the lead while you drive behind."

9.

They got to the house a few minutes later. A gateman opened the gate and she drove in. It was a three-bedroom duplex with a study which she had converted to a fourth room for her domestic help. A fence divided the other tenant. She had sent the girl away when there were speculations that she was diabolic and when she started noticing certain changes. She planned to get someone else. Only the governor and the ADC went inside the house. She brought out plastic chairs and placed them on the verandah for them to sit when she realized it was probably the protocol to stay outside. She offered him a seat and asked Nene to serve the guests with water first and then drinks while she prepared the meal. Luckily, she hadn't put the soups in the deep freezer yet as she only cooked them that evening having left work early to do so before leaving to the church by

6.30pm. She would only need a little while to prepare the swallow, as they preferred to eat *poundo*.

"Excellency you have made my sister's day, I must tell you. Her best moment is when she watches people eat her food with pleasure. She is always inviting her choir and church members for one thing or the other so she could serve them a meal. I am sure she was going to invite them down to celebrate my safe arrival. Her own is food ministry," she said with a giggle.

"Interesting. So, this actually turns out to be a celebration of my safe landing," he said soberly. He turned to the ADC. "I want photographs taken of this little gathering. Invite everyone inside for this shall be a memorial of my mortality and vulnerability."

"I am not dressed for photographs o," Eka said and made to rush into the kitchen.

"No no no. Please stay. I want us to capture this moment in its ordinariness. You are dressed enough." She then excused the governor, asking Nene to join her in the kitchen.

"So where did Eka get this gift of hospitality?" the governor asked, seeing how radiant and pleased Eka was looking as she set down the food flasks. He could see through that she wasn't flattered by his company, there was just a genuine desire to please, to serve and it didn't seem to matter who was at the receiving end.

"Ask her o."

Eka smiled shyly and said. "I realized so early that I loved to cook. But then I had quite a small capacity to eat. And of what use is food if it is not eaten? So, I would always find excuses to invite people over and would be sooo happy just knowing they were enjoying the food."

"You don't charge them?"

"Nooo. Not at all. I have been blessed so early. I just see it as my way of paying back. I schooled under a scholarship for both bachelors and master's degrees at Cambridge and Harvard and got a good job immediately after youth service. I tried marriage and it didn't work. I have an eight-year-old kid whose father took custody of when he turned seven. I have no strength to fight so as Nene has said, my own is food ministry. It's my own way of getting people together and exercising my humanity and keeping my sanity. " She laughed. "Sometimes I feel guilty when my choir people come over because it seems I am using them for my joy because I become so elated when they eat my food and it would seem I was exploiting them."

"No no no no," the governor said, not realizing when he stood up and walked towards her as she was wiping the plates. "It's fine. Here you are feeling guilty for deriving joy from serving people who give you nothing in return and yet there are some of us planning to derive joy in taking over what belongs to the people. Please allow yourself to enjoy your joy for such a joy is a blessing and I am really blessed to meet someone like you." He spontaneously spread his arms and hugged her. "Thank you for your humanity," he said. And then as if he was about rendering a speech, he turned to no one in particular and said, "You see… after today's experience, only a foolish man would not reflect on his life. I saw death. But do we need near tragic experiences to wake us up to our common humanity? Do we need a near plane crash to remind us that we are here today and should make the best of it not just for ourselves but especially for others? I don't think so." And then he turned to Nene. "And by the way Nene thanks for your message for it helped me to redirect my focus. What I want you to do for me is this. I want you to be my pulse feeler. Your job would be to mix up with people both young and old and find out what they are saying about my government and what their expectations are and you are to communicate your findings to me without sugar coating them, weekly. You will be trained on putting these matters in infographics. You shall travel in the local beaten-down taxis, the rickety buses, the motor bikes and sit around in motor parks and bars and restaurants and all you do is listen. You shall learn to generate discussions with people that would help you sift their opinions. You shall conduct opinion polls with NGOs and speak with business people. It shall be like a secret service. You shall swear an oath of confidentiality like all of them here have done. I do not want people in the streets knowing you as an appointee of the governor but you shall have my ears, you shall be part of my inner caucus, you shall call my attention and be my conscience. Do you understand?" She nodded and was opening her mouth to affirm when he followed with the question. "Do you think you can do that for me and for the people of our state?"

" I am really flattered sir. I think I can and I will do my very best. This shows you are a good leader because you are not afraid of feedback. Others treat feedback with disdain and even persecute those who criticize them. But you are actually searching for feedback!" Then out of a sudden she became quite emotional and dramatic. She knelt down and raised her hands up "May the Lord bless you and protect you from all harm, may he give you wisdom and great joy in serving his people, may your reward be in the many lives you will see transformed and who will bless you, may your heritage be like David's which would last forever..." They were at a loss as to what to do as she sobbed until she started saying "Thank you Jesus. Thank you Jesus" and sat up slowly.

"Ah Excellency lucky you o! Nene went into a prayerful trance for you? Me here I have been waiting for ages, " Eka said.

"What's that? " The governor asked curiously.

"You didn't know ? From childhood she used to have this wave in which she would speak into someone's life and his fortunes would change. People used to seek her out for prayers up till when she was seventeen. Now she don spoil," Eka said jokingly.

"Big Sis stop na."

"I surprise o. Means the thing has come back again and it will soon be my turn." They laughed. He laughed too but the curiosity lingered. Maybe, just maybe, God had pushed this girl his way to be his angel. After all it was said that God worked in mysterious ways. He would have to add to all her other tasks an intercessory role. There was always a God factor in things, that unexplainable reason why something succeeded in spite of all the fears and all the blunders or why something failed despite all the meticulous planning. He would have to factor it in everything he did. Whereas the average Nigerian sat back and depended on God and did nothing else, the difference in his own case would be that he would plan and work as if everything depended on himself and then pray as though everything depended on the supernatural. *Laborare est orare.* He would so work hard that his work would become a prayer while his prayer would be a thanksgiving arising from his work. He would so work hard that those of his colleagues who were lazy and only after vanities would be rattled and start performing when they saw the mileage his state had put in. From now on he would make the state resources work for the people. He would see himself as if he were 'president' of one of those small African countries and institute whatever measures would make life enviable for citizens of his state.

Bullshit federal government! As long as he was not yet dead, as long as this life of his remained a gift, he would use it to dignify everyone in his state, especially those who had no one else to stand up for them. When people prayed "Give us this day our daily bread…" his government would be that agency God would use to answer their prayer. He would prove to the world that the black politician was not incurably selfish.

BOOK THREE

LOAVES OF BODIES

1.

"Thank God for the break," he said to himself, quickly packing his files and putting them in his carry-on bag. "I am really tired." He took the escalator to the fifth floor of the UN Headquarters building to have a bite at the restaurant. He spotted a colleague from Kenya and walked up to her and quickly placed his bag on an empty seat beside her and went to queue to pay for food. The restaurant was open to both UN staff and visitors.

"How did your session go?" Margaret asked as he took a bite. He raised his head and his eyes caught her hair as he masticated the stewed meat. Her hair was straight and unadorned yet beautifully black and shiny. He recalled that hardly had he seen these East Africans go crazy about hair the way Nigerian ladies spent humungous amounts for fake flowing hair.

"It was depressing." He took another spoonful. "Frankly I get embarrassed when I attend these sessions on new forms of slavery. The cycle is just being repeated all over."

"What cycle ?"

"The slave trade. Only that this time our governments are the enablers. They are making sure every young man and woman runs away from home under any guise. They walk into it unknowingly of course, in a bid to escape the corruption induced extreme poverty only to be bound by a chain of lies and exploitation."

"And when their eyes open it is always too late, for then they are either dried out in the deserts as meat for vultures or bloated at sea as loaves of bodies," Margaret added.

"Yeah. Only yesterday, a boat with more than twenty dead bodies of Nigerian women and girls was arrested. Not to mention those who simply drown and nobody gets to identify their bodies."

Margaret was checking her watch as he spoke. "Tragic. I am afraid I will have to leave for the next session. Did you say you were going to Rome today ? Safe trip then." She patted him on the back and left hurriedly.

He was done for the day. He didn't sign up for another session because he knew he would be traveling. He would have to go down to one of the lounges and find a place to relax for a while.

He was lucky to find a vacant seat at the Qatar Lounge. The chair was ornate as a throne, with a golden lavish vanish. He adjusted and sat comfortably. Right from childhood he was conscious of being teased that he had a female backside. He knew that if he were ever crazy enough to become a cross-dresser, he wouldn't be lacking of a good fundament.

Across the glass screen, he had a good view of the East River. In the distance it looked darkish green and ever-flowing and un-finishing, with gentle and swaying waves, as if all it could do was nourish life and never take it. A helicopter flew past. It looked tiny in the horizon and unhurried like a buzzing laidback fly.

He dozed.

He heard himself snoring and woke up with a start. Nearby was another man who was snoring in high pitches. He felt like going to tap him to adjust his position. He learnt that lying sideways helped people who snored. He checked his watch. He would need to walk towards First Avenue before ordering Uber to take him to Queens to board his flight. He had already checked out of the hotel.

He took one last look at the East River across the glass screen and was lost in thought for a brief moment. Flowing waters had that elixir of sobriety. He was just an ordinary civil society representative but there were times he wished he held the power to make things happen. These conferences were good for people with good political will but it seemed to him that in his country, as soon as a man was elected or appointed into a governmental position, he became partially blind, seeing only himself.

2.

Fiumicino.

They just landed. The duty-free shops seemed to stretch endlessly as he searched for the immigration hall. It was a bit confusing with the renovations going on but thank God, all a traveler needed to do was follow the directions provided. He was wondering what the hurry was with these passengers when it dawned on him that they wanted to be the firsts to be cleared by immigration. He added some brisk to his steps. It was too late, the hall was filled to capacity. It was nondescript, bereft of any aesthetical efforts to make it look welcoming probably because of the renovations. It seemed somewhat contracted, hardly enough for the huge traffic that arrived Rome daily. This was a bad hour to arrive, as people inched forward shoulder to shoulder to where their passports would be stamped. The contrast was amazing. Only two and a half hours earlier they had left a chill of 14 degrees in London, as he had first flown into London before embarking to Rome, and now, though outside temperatures may be 20, right here, inside this hall, with all these masses of boiling bodies, it could be anything from 120 degrees Celsius!

What made it worse was that the line was as fast as a snail. Was there any air-conditioning here at all? He did not need to look around to confirm, just that it couldn't comply with these human generators. There were at least a thousand persons in the hall, each inching his way forward. But this heat wasn't something he had bargained for in an industrialized nation. This wasn't any different from Lagos. Lagos meant high temperatures, chaos, high decibel noises, sweat and strain. This wasn't much different except for the decibels.

Ten minutes were like forever. No progress. Only a swirling babel from the subdued conversations. He scanned the crowds. Majority seemed Chinese. Or maybe Japanese or Korean. He couldn't seem to distinguish them. Then he slipped away, conscious only of the song that played in his mind.

A slap on his wrist woke him up.

"What are you trying to do?" the man shouted.

A thousand eyes were on him. His mouth was agape, his brain trying to process the embarrassing scene.

"I am sorry. I don't know. I was just playing."

"Playing with my wallet? You pick pocket!"

"Pick pocket!" he retorted aloud unbelievably staring at the man completely confounded. *Pick pocket*, as in petty thief? 'Me a thief? A common thief in a crowded hall like this?' he wondered quickly. He was too dazed and short of words.

Polizia arrived immediately and he was led away for possible interrogation. Two men who had been next in line were invited too. He prayed the ground should open and just swallow him up than bearing this shame. Before the episode he had even glanced around and seen that he was the only black person. What made it even more terrible was that he held a green passport, a document outstanding in its notoriety in international circles.

The police seized his passport temporarily as they were led into an office. An immigrations police officer took the passport away. His heart was pounding. He had never stolen, well…except when as a kid he took his mother's change. Which kid didn't do that? It was always your mum's… But to say he was a thief, a pick pocket… My goodness! Where did that come from? He must have woken up from the wrong side this morning.

"You speak Italian ?"

"Solo English," he responded.

"Ok. I speak small. My colleague will handle this." He brought out a phone and dialed a number and spoke in that characteristically fast and musical style that is Italian, and less than a minute another police officer walked briskly in. It was a lady.

He said a quick prayer. "Come oh Holy Spirit fill the heart of thy faithful. And enkindle in me the fire of thy love … Oh God who did instruct the heart of thy faithful by the gift of the Holy Spirit, grant that by the gift of the same Holy Spirit, I may truly be wise and ever rejoice in His divine consolation. Through Christ our Lord. Amen."

Somehow his confidence got a boost.

"What happened?" the police officer enquired staring straight into his eyes.

"As we were on the queue, my colleague called my attention to the fact that this man was trying to open my sling wallet. I turned and saw his hand on it and slapped his wrist." His English was accented, so he could be Croatian or Macedonian. He seemed to be in his late 30s.

"Yes. I saw him fiddling with the cover of the pouch as if he was trying to open it."

They had taken his landing card from him.

He saw the immigrations official returning with his passport and landing card. They spoke for a while in Italian, and he noticed her growing confusion. He hoped this was positive. He had never been this embarrassed.

"Now tell me what you say happened. Why were you fiddling with his pouch?" She had become gentler even though quite serious.

His eyes moistened. His voice trembled.

"Honestly I don't know what happened. I just want to say that I have been travelling all over the world and have never committed any offence. In my country I don't have any criminal record. I think I was just distracted and became absent minded because of the long wait and just began to fiddle with things around. I wasn't even aware that I was doing that. Please believe me that I had no criminal intentions whatsoever."

"Why are you here in Rome?"

"I am attending a conference organized by the Vatican. "

"We need to see your invitation letter and confirm from the Vatican."

"Ok. But I would need Wi-Fi. I could forward it to an email address of your choice."

"You are supposed to have every document on demand."

"Yes. And again, I am sorry. These days we hardly print these things, and I am a frequent traveler. I was here in March. I have never engaged in anything criminal in all my travels. If you check my passport you will see that I travel around a lot. My visa still has a validity period of three months…"

"24 hours are long enough for anyone to change. Maybe you just haven't been caught before. Saints don't carry an ID you know. Nor criminals," the lady officer said, smiling but dead serious. A smile was always a window even if unintended. He knew he must cash in on it.

 He was quiet. This was one of those times home became a literal metaphor for paradise. If there was anything he wanted in all his life, at this moment, it was to be in Paradise, home. It was strange how when things got complicated simple things one took for granted became grand desires.

 Another police officer came in. He spoke to her in Italian and she stood up and left the room shortly. "You wait here," she said. They were left alone.

He turned to his accuser. "My brother…"

"I am not your brother," the man interjected. He just wanted to bring him to an understanding before the officers returned. Making peace was crucial even if he was let off or prosecuted.

"I am really sorry about this. I have never stolen. I preach against stealing. I am a Catholic priest. I could be accused of other things but not stealing, least of all pick pocketing! Please. I think I was only fiddling with things around."

The man, whom he heard the police officer address as Petros stood up suddenly and began to scream. "You are a priest. A thieving priest. You fiddle with children. You fiddle with men and now you fiddle with my pouch…" The Police man was stern in his warning and calmed him down. "Why you not dress in collar ? You are priest? So you could fiddle…Fiddler…Pedophile."

He reasoned there must be more to it. Either Petros had been abused at childhood by a priest and this was an opportunity for vengeance or he was venting his feelings against all the scandals of the pedophilia he had heard over the news. Yes. Why hadn't he worn his clerical shirt? The collar was a sign, a sign of his poverty as a priest, of his transparency and identity. Even if he had several of them because of hygiene, yet that stability and regularity of colour, black or grey or white, was a statement against ostentation, vanity. So why hadn't he worn it?

The female police officer returned. This was like half an hour afterwards.

"I have watched the cameras. We have taken it from various angles and we see that he wasn't furtive about it. It's not showing whether he tried to open the button or not. The camera didn't capture him as taking anything from your bag. It would be quite foolish for anyone to try to steal here when everything is under CCTV.

"As none of your items is missing, and as we cannot clearly say he had intentions of stealing, I am afraid we cannot press any charges. We will have to let him go."

A bucketful of gratitude splashed across his heart. Petros left and gave him a stern resentful look. He could only stare back, bewildered, yet with eyes seeking understanding.

"Why you didn't wear your clerical shirt. Why?" The Policewoman asked, now intently, staring at him. He had to force himself to stare back. He didn't like staring back at people. He preferred looking away, locking eyes briefly and looking away again. Somehow for Westerners, it was seen as a sign of a deficit of confidence. When there was no harm in being himself, he preferred to look away as he talked. Actually, he preferred to just close his eyes, spewing out his responses, as if they came from a mental bank that only opened with locked eyes. But if he met people of other cultures, he scorched them with his gaze.

He kept his gaze fixed on her.

"It's more convenient to travel incognito. There's so much resentment towards priests in the West with the pedophilia controversies. I just want to be seen as a normal human being. I don't want people making judgments about me as soon as they see me."

She regarded him for a moment.

"Well. I am gonna let you go because, technically, you have not committed any crime. And I can't even establish an intention here to commit one. But I want to advise that you see a psychologist."

He looked at her in surprise, his eyes seeking more explanation.

"You seem distracted. It's a lonely life I know. My brother is a priest. You guys are lonely and it could get into you. It could make you mindless. So, take my advice. See a psychologist."

"Thank you. I mean, for letting me go. I sincerely had no intention to embarrass myself."

"I know. But take me seriously. The way you looked on CCTV, you were completely unaware of what you were doing. You will need help with a professional."

"Thank you. I will take your advice."

"You promise?" She asked surprisingly burning her gaze right into him.

"I do." He said, with a bit of discomfort. He was sensing that part of the condition for letting him go was that promise he had made. It was a subtle sentence though without a court ruling. He was grateful she let him go, for these immigration officials were empowered to send visitors right back with the next available flight. Was there something about the brother who was a priest that was informing her decision and her insistence to extract a promise from him to seek help? And he had made the promise. It didn't matter that she wouldn't be there to monitor him. A promise was a self-binding imperative. It didn't matter whether any other person was there to witness its fulfillment. An integrity gap was created as soon as a promise was made. The more one broke promises the larger the deficit of trust, leading to a withering in reputation and credibility. He didn't want to push himself to a point in which he would not trust himself anymore, the way politicians had lost all self-trust.

3.

He did not enjoy the trip. It was an International Labour Organization supported event on Decent Work. ILO had taken upon itself to promote Goal 8 of the Sustainable Development Goals and was building a coalition across the world to promote job creation for youths and vulnerable groups. The event was being hosted at the Rome Global Gateway villa, a campus of the Notre Dame University, Indiana, located on Via Ostilia in the Rione Celio neighbourhood on the slopes of the Caelian Hill.

The main attraction was that the campus was located a block away from the Coliseum. He had always seen the Coliseum at a distance, being driven past by bus or tram but now there was great opportunity to stand by it and admire the ancient architecture. He never stopped wondering at such engineering feats with such low technology as they had. But then the truth was that those were the heights of their civilizations. Each civilization reached heights which future ones looked back and wondered how they were accomplished, mistakenly evaluating past feats with present lenses whereas those were products of the highest existing know-how.

He wasn't paying attention to the presentations. The conference hall had a capacity to sit up to seventy persons. There were no tables for participants, only chairs with built in wooden writing pads. The hall had two projector screens that rolled up to the ceiling when not in use. They had been told to not bother with taking notes as the presentations would be mailed to them. He didn't like hearing that, for it automatically made him pay less attention. Whenever he took notes, he understood the subject better. His mind kept drawing him back to the episode at the airport and his promise to see a professional. What if they had insisted on keeping the benefit of the doubt? That means they would have branded him a suspect and splashed his face on the press and he would be detained, awaiting trial. Or put in the next available plane and sent back home. 'God forbid!' He exclaimed.

"What ?"

"Oh nothing," he answered in embarrassment. He didn't know he had spoken out aloud. A few heads turned and looked his way. He felt very uncomfortable.

"You alright?" The lady sitting on his right whispered. She was Egyptian. She had introduced herself as running an ecumenical NGO that worked with a major Muslim organization providing skills for youths in the rural areas.

"Yeah. I am. I guess. Thank you."

His attention got worse. Now he was wondering about how he would be perceived by other participants especially those who sat close to him, and he was wearing his priest collar.

'Maybe I should really see a professional or just talk to someone,' he said to himself. The problem was that as a Priest he saw himself as invincible. He never believed he would come to a stage where anyone would suggest to him to seek professional help; rather his role was always to be a succor, to be a transformer, to listen and to bless. This situation was like the hunter being hunted. Could there be any other priests, carrying pains, burdens, ailments around because they believed they were too strong to be stricken; and people believed in that myth of invincibility, until there was total breakdown? He had once visited a priest at the psychiatric hospital and wondered how it got to that point. How come nobody noticed and drew attention ? Maybe it started like this ?

It was lunch break.

The meal was set up in the open courtyard, with the mild spring sun radiating. There were two serving spots, flanked by seats under the trees and unshaded tables directly under the rays. He left his queue to join the other. There was a Sikh from Germany who was attending the event as well. He was the last man on the queue. They dished their food and went over to one of the unshaded tables. The Sikh man introduced himself as Jabraj. He was probably in his mid-forties and spoke in German accented English. He was quite restrained in his mannerism and had this calm mien that disconcerted one momentarily. He was about 1.72ft and made taller by his head gear which was a bit of mismatch with his trendy suit and tie. He had well-trimmed moustache that rounded well into his beards.

"I have always been curious to know why you wear the pointed turban," he said smiling and having a bite of the lasagna.

"Oh this?" Jabraj said touching the head gear. "It's a reminder to us that there is something always above us to look towards so we don't live below and forget about what is above."

"Wow. Great. How strange it is that we see these symbols every day and never care to find out their meaning."

"That is true. There would be a lot achieved and nothing to lose if the various religions make attempts to understand one other at least," he said and went on to talk about the efforts in Germany, and how government had created the space for interaction between the religions and how this was helping create awareness and contain stigma and prejudice.

"I chair the group of all the religions. We meet and we dialogue on common issues, we are realizing that there is more that unites than divides. You know I have made it a point to study all the major religions. Basically, their founders wanted peace for mankind. All founders without exception. No religion preaches hatred for mankind as its doctrine. But practitioners have turned things upside down and made religion a cause of division instead of harmony."

"Well, the good thing is that great efforts are going on at the same time, trying to create common grounds. By the way let me hear from a Sikh himself. What are you all about?"

"You could have asked Google you know," he said, laughing. "Anyways. Just kidding." He went on to talk about the life cycle of human beings, where karma guides birth, life and rebirth. Sikhs didn't believe in death sort of, just the recycling of life. "So, we don't believe in a physical heaven or hell. When you are happy, that is heaven and when you suffer that is hell. The one God of Sikhs is the same God of all religions. Sikhs believe the various religions are only a path to worshipping the one God. And Christianity believes that this God was incarnate in Jesus the Christ. He took flesh and dwelt among men and sacrificed himself for the salvation of humankind," he added without prompting, with a smile. "But I never really get to understand the salvation part. Why does God need to die?" he asked, genuinely curious.

The question threw Fr. Itanja a bit off balance. He must say the man was quite articulate and held his beliefs passionately and could communicate them well. But he hadn't expected him to throw a question back at him.

"God just wanted to show that love is sacrifice. We call it the Atonement. It is a great sign of love, that God would stop at nothing; not even the life of His Son would be too precious to hold Him back, He would be ready to sacrifice it to bring humankind back to a life of harmony with him. That is Redemption. Christians believe that what caused a setback originally between God and humankind is redeemed through the Death and Resurrection of Jesus the Christ, and not only are we restored into friendship, we are also made into God's adopted children."

"Fantastic. But do your adherents really believe they have become children of God?"

"You mean by their actions? Otherwise it's a gift you receive through baptism…"

He couldn't continue because the facilitator signaled everyone to go in for the second session. He hurried over his coffee and thrashed the plastic spoon.

As he sat back during the session, his mind kept wandering back to what Jagraj had said about there being no real heaven nor hell. If so it meant only 20% of the world's 7.7 billion people were in some kind of heaven, with about 5% in a super heaven and about a billion persons in the darkest hell, with the remaining oscillating between a mild hell and a peripheral heaven. Well, maybe things balanced up with the karma. But what was a man's business if he was born and never knew he had lived a previous life? Even with a belief that after death would come judgment his countrymen lived as if there was no form of accountability after this life; how much more this kind of religion that taught no heaven nor hell in the afterlife but a cycle of rebirths! He was sure that his countrymen would simply multiply their nefarious acts claiming that it wouldn't concern them since they would be reborn several times anyway and they wouldn't even know they were the ones from a previous life!

He traced his paper with meaningless darts, the way he did whenever he was physically present but mentally elsewhere.

He was sure that many of his countrymen just mouthed beliefs and filled the churches and mosques every week but correlated few of those eternal truths with their moral choices. Religion was more or less a ritual of worship. Otherwise how would a politician believe in judgment in the afterlife and still steal a whole nation dry in order to accumulate wealth he and his family could never exhaust in a million generations? He was convinced that secretly the political class believed in the immortality of the body and not of the soul.

The Egyptian lady was a Coptic Christian. He couldn't place her age for as someone had said, 'women and wine should not be dated'. But there was something about her looks that showed she was a grandma of sorts. She was a bit stout, compensating for a height which didn't really suppress her as short. She hurriedly tapped him on the shoulder as the session was over. "Please wait for me. I need to use the restroom. I need to ask you for a favour."

"Okay." He rummaged through his mind wondering

the kind of favour she would ask. He had barely spoken to her, more so because his outburst made him curl a bit like an embarrassed dog. Maybe she needed to be put through some of the concepts ? Or maybe…His mind went everywhere. 'Why not just wait,' he counselled himself. 'The woman will be here in a moment!'

For a moment he realized that this was his past time, projecting about things he could patiently wait to get the answers. He so often worried about minutiae that he got no time to really enjoy the present. People were still chatting. Most participants had moved to the courtyard. There had been a suggestion that the group take a walk to the Coliseum and then to the Basilica of St. Agnes for a mass. He had celebrated his mass in the morning as soon as he woke up. He found it quite difficult to discipline himself to pray in the evening. As a priest he needed to pray the lauds, the office of the reading, the midday prayer, the vespers and the night prayers. He would wake up and pray all of them at once, justifying that the prayers were directed towards God who was not restricted by time.

The woman caught up with him.

"It's really nothing," she said, seeing his anxious looks. "There is an Italian restaurant I visited ten years ago with my husband during our anniversary. I wanted to ask if you would join me for dinner there as I wouldn't want to go alone. It is in the Transtevere area."

He smiled with relief.

"Of course. No problem. I will gladly accompany you." He knew what that meant. Back in Nigeria if someone invited you out, you knew they were going to pay. But when in Rome you did as the Romans did. In fact, when he didn't know what was meant by being invited out by friends for a night out he got himself thoroughly embarrassed by accepting an invitation by a group of his mates when he did a short course in Brussels. They ate and drank and the bill came. He was shocked when everyone was counting out his own portion to pay. He was sweating heavily. He quickly had to make up a story about forgetting his wallet and asked a colleague to loan him some money to pay. He made the refunds as soon as they got back to the hotel. Since then, if anyone asked him for an evening out he feigned busyness. He however found this quite fascinating because it meant that friends didn't mount pressure on others. If you wanted to drink you bought your own drink and if you wanted to eat you paid for it. This way expectations were clear and well managed. Accepting this woman's invitation now meant that he was ready to spend a tidy sum, eating. In any case he had cured himself of that predilection to quickly mentally convert Euro into his local currency before making any expenditure. The money was always too much. He did that a lot and realized that he would never enjoy his visits overseas, as long as he kept on lamenting how much naira went into the purchase of a single item when converted. In the past he starved sometimes, knowing that eating one good meal in Europe could feed a whole family back home in Nigeria. Now he just spent the money he had and not give a thought to it. What did his people say? *The one you put into your stomach was your real gift.* What would all these struggles amount to if one could not have one decent meal!

"My husband passed away five years ago," she said as they walked out of the premises.

Rome was full of one-ways and narrow ancient streets. Cars as tiny as match boxes lined the streets everywhere. He realized that in Rome the smaller the car the better, as there were hardly any parking spaces and the available ones were quite expensive. Many people preferred to leave their vehicles at home and commute through the trams.

"I am so sorry about that. May his soul rest in peace."

"Amen."

4.

They took a cab through the ancient windy streets and got to their destination thirty minutes later. By Roman standards it was still too early for dinner and so they strolled around a bit and stood by the Trevi Fountain among little crowds of people watching a performance by a man who had made musical instruments out of wine bottles. Rome was always a flux of people. In many of the meetings he attended here, right up till 11pm they would still be at dinner, with the Italians and Spaniards talking at the top of their voices, eating one set of meal after another. You always knew the meal was over when they served you coffee.

The restaurant was a beehive. Apparently she had booked a table for two, as they were ushered in to a corner with a view to the street. They were approached by a waiter for their orders. He went first for water and then red wine. There was a small basket of bread served with a sauce of olive oil and balsam as they waited for the *apperitivo*. Unlike the palatable bread they always had back home for breakfast, here there were all kinds of bread, for breakfast, lunch, dinner. The *apperitivo* was a cold meal consisting of a snack with crostini, some cold cuts, cheese and bruschetta.

His eyes caught Hannah observing him. "I am sorry I interrupted your plans," she said. "I am delighted that you didn't mind coming with me."

"Oh no. No worries at all. It's alright. It's actually nice leaving the crowd and coming out by ourselves." The waiter returned and poured some more wine into his glass. They had ordered a full bottle. The *apperitivo* was meant to prepare their stomachs. For a moment he marveled at how alcohol had become a religious taboo in some traditions. Muslims didn't drink it and many Christian denominations saw it as too worldly to be indulged in. He believed personally that if one could stay away from alcohol it was a good decision but he knew quite well that his scriptures condemned drunkenness not alcohol itself. Of course the wine served at the wedding feast in Cana attended by Jesus was not fruit juice.

"By the way since it's your anniversary, the dinner is on me," he said, in an attempt to be chivalrous.

"Oh no. Seriously," she said with a blush. "I want to pay for this. I invited you the African way," she said laughing. "I insist."

"Okay then."

The *il primo,* the first hot meal, was served. It was the usual pasta. He smiled as he recalled the Italian taxi driver who made fun of Chinese people with their "every time reese! reese!!" until it struck him that he was referring to rice. 'But Italiano pasta! Pasta!! Pasta!!!' he teased the driver, to which he shrugged as if to say pasta was normal but rice was not. It just went to show how people accommodated their own idiosyncrasies and looked down on others. The *secondo* would be meat or fish served with *il contorno* or side dish of vegetable or salad and lastly sweets or fruits, with a final cup of coffee. He never failed to observe that while the Italians cooked their meals piecemeal and served as different courses they in *Ejaghamland* put it together and served as one main meal. He chuckled as he observed that his people had a simple culture of one straight meal which the Italians subdivided into courses. But he agreed that the Italians knew a lot about relating over food.

"I have a confession to make," she said suddenly, smiling, "and I hope you don't take offense."

His heart sank a bit. No wonder she had eaten mostly in silence, sometimes regarding him through the corner of her eyes and when their eyes met would smile. She had carefully allowed him to complete the main meal before raising whatever the issue was, for his appetite had suddenly cut.

"Do I need to wear my stole?" he asked jokingly. Priests always wore a purple stole to hear a penitent's confession.

"No no. It's not a sacramental confession. You see I invited you because I wanted to talk to you. I know you are a priest and you are used to talking to people who have issues. I know that sometimes priests forget themselves and do not realize they need to take care of themselves. I felt moved to ask you whether you are having any challenges that you need to share. At least you may never see me again so my presence won't remind you of the interaction. In short, how can I be of help?"

For a moment he was disconcerted. He threw a

glance around the room and saw mostly couples eating and talking excitedly in Italian. There was a family with a boy running around the whole place and the mum making great effort to ensure he didn't trip or cause much havoc. She would follow him without restraining him, unless he latched on to something that was potentially dangerous. Whenever he attended Holy Mass on Sundays during his travels he noticed that parents allowed their kids to roam free without any restraint. Back home in Nigeria parents would hold their kids in check in a constant struggle. He sometimes wondered whether that was the origin of de-initiation, where African children lost some of their God-given initiatives out of undue restraint.

He was sincerely touched and overwhelmed by her offer.

"It's about my mum," he said simply, remaining silent for a while, overcome with emotion. She raised an eyebrow as if to say 'What about her?' and then looked away, knowing that he would talk in his own time. He took a drink from the glass of water. Even as he cleared his throat he was still slightly choked.

"I came home to learn my mum was sick. I work in a different city about 700 miles away. I was told she didn't want to go to the hospital so I went and practically forced her. She was on admission for two days when she insisted she wanted to be discharged. I think she was concerned that a lot of money was being spent. You know our mothers, they want to give all and take nothing, they don't want you to be broke because of them. In my country health insurance is for a few. But really money wasn't an issue at all, I was happy to spend for my mum to get well. The doctor advised us to keep her overnight for observation and I practically forced her to spend another night against her will. I was supposed to go back that night to see her but on my way, I got a call from a longtime friend. She was someone I admired a lot and had tried hard when we were growing up for us to be friends but always met a brick wall. I hadn't heard from her for years so when she called to say she was in town and had heard I was in town too and wanted us to meet I just agreed without thinking. I turned the car around and went over to see her. It was just nothing other than the excitement of being with her after so many years," he said with a smile. "We went out for a drink and talked about old times till it was quite late for me to go back to the hospital. Or so I thought. It was kind of romantic though and something I thought had suppressed reared its head somehow. We nearly did it that night."

"Did what?" She asked with a mischievous smile.

"I nearly broke my celibate commitment."

"What! You nearly proposed to her?"

"You are being naughty," he said laughing. "No. I mean that I nearly asked her to spend the night with me. Somehow, I saw that she wouldn't have minded, despite my being a priest. At the end I had to very weakly resist the temptation and drop her off. I could still have gone to see my mum even though it was late but I put it off till the next morning and went home to sleep.

'Very early in the morning, around 5am my brother-in-law drove to the family house and was honking, making a noise that early. I didn't need to ask him why he came; he had never visited at that hour. I knew mama had died." He paused and was now shedding tears profusely. He couldn't talk anymore as he was choked. He breathed in and out heavily, constantly wiping off the tears that rolled down his cheeks. "I missed the chance of seeing my mother one last time before she departed, because of a woman! If I had listened to her to take her home she probably would still be alive…"

And now the tears were uncontrollable.

Hannah allowed him his space. Sometimes it was better to allow a man to cry, to feel weak and appear vulnerable. Sometimes a man's tears were like a rare syrup that was bottled up and now needed for a cure. Sometimes that was all that was needed to clear the head, to peel off the layer of fog that had clouded the vision.

"So sorry to hear about that. When did this happen?"

"Six months ago," he managed to say, wiping his tears.

She sat quietly for a long while. Very softly music was playing in the background. It featured an Italian tenor but it was muffled by the chatter. He wasn't much into music and artists and wouldn't know who it was. But some comfort came with the song as it managed to sear through the dissonance and get to his soul. Sharing this story brought a measure of relief. Otherwise his heart usually cut even in the midst of a dream and he would wake up with a start, breathing heavily as he would pass through yet another spasm of guilt exclaiming "Oh mme! Oh mme!!"

"I am really sorry about that," Hannah said again. "But I think you have to forgive yourself. When my husband died I was away on a trip and carried the guilt for two years until I read a book which helped to calm me down. Of course, I prayed a lot too. I don't need to tell you about prayer. Do I? But one thing I came to learn was to separate the hard facts from those ones sexed up by my mind. I have learnt to realize that I am different from my mind and I should be in control of it, not be under its control. The mind sexes things up a lot. It exaggerates, it raises unnecessary dimensions to an issue, complicates and magnifies it above the actual reality. So, what I do now is that I just separate the reality from the imaginative capacity of my mind. For instance, in my own case I accepted the reality that I was away and had no way of knowing he was going to die. I stopped blaming myself for what was out of my control. If I were you I would accept the fact that I was distracted from seeing my mum because of an old friend and because I thought I would see mum the next morning. I would accept the fact that well, I am not God to have known that she would die that night. I would accept that she died anyway and there was nothing I could do about that. Yes, I couldn't see her before she died. That was bad enough. But then there is nothing I can do now about it. So, if there is nothing I can do about it, I shouldn't worry about it because it won't change anything. You know when my husband died my mind kept telling me I killed him because I wasn't there for him and I accepted its stupid verdict. Then after I wizened up I would retort and say Liar! Of course, I got better not because I called my mind names but because I simply accepted the reality of his death and stopped allowing my mind to play games with me. If I can do something about something then I do it. If I cannot do something about something, I just let it go because I just can't do anything about it. So, I guess you would have to stop blaming yourself. Stop worrying and live fully in the present. The mind takes our attention away from the present and fills us with dreadful images or guilt from the past or fears or visions or wonderful ideas about the future and we end up being mediocre at the present task because our attention is divided between the past and the future. So just be here and excel. Never allow your mind mess up your date with the moment," she said smiling.

Maybe because it was totally unexpected or maybe because he did not expect such direct flow of concern, the words hit him pleasantly like a cool breeze on a warm afternoon. He felt a surge of relief, that feeling that takes over when you had no more a care in the world, when you suddenly realized you had been worrying yourself over nothing. And he wondered how many people had been left to deteriorate because their minds held them hostage and no one wanted to be called an intruder.

But he knew all these things Hannah had said to him. So why hadn't he talked to himself, why hadn't he listened to himself ? Why was it that it more often had to take another to console?

5.

Two months passed.

He was going through his emails that Tuesday morning when he saw a reminder about a meeting in Geneva. He thought he had already responded and sent his details for hotel and flight bookings. He really needed to improve on self-management. The meeting was only a month away. He quickly rummaged his office bag for his passport, to check the validity of his visa. The visa was still valid but would expire a day after the conference! What if something happened, like missing his flight for whatever reason and he had to stay back? He would then be the subject of unnecessary immigration protocols. It was dangerous. As there was still a one-month window, he decided to try his luck with getting his visa renewed. He had always had the luck of having a one-year visa issued to him by the Italian Embassy. He had traveled to Rome so many times that he had no fear at all about being rejected. For many priests like him the Schengen visa from Italy was the best bet. Although the regulation was that you should get the visa from a country you would visit the longest, sometimes, depending on the meetings one had to attend, it was always better to get the Schengen from Italy.

He would quickly have to download an Italian Embassy form and complete it if indeed he wanted his visa within the month.

Two years earlier he could get a visa without even an invitation letter. All he needed was a cover letter from the papal Nuncio, the Vatican Ambassador. Now he would not only have to obtain an Invitation letter, he would provide his bank statement with a cover letter from the bank, a letter of introduction from his employers, show evidence of flight reservation and hotel reservation, travel health insurance, a bio data sheet, a passport photo, and the mother of them all, a yellow fever card issued not later than a year earlier! He wasn't sure when his card was dated, but he remembered he had been on a trip to Cote D'Ivoire when he was asked for the yellow card at the immigrations and he had none to present. He was charged seven thousand naira for the vaccine and given the yellow card. Would he now have to take another vaccine to update the card if it was older than one year? He lamented at the fact that Nigerians had made Europe a superior heaven and in spite of their apparent religiosity, had downgraded the real Heaven. The desperation youths displayed to go to Europe gave it credence as some paradise, and Europe used the prospect to strangulate them with conditions so stringent that going to the real Heaven was less cumbersome. And so, to side step the mines, they drowned at sea after being scorched at the desert, with many simply dying without a funeral. The various governments that ruled Nigeria clearly showed that the black man had not yet matured to the status of citizenship. He remembered reading a write up on citizenship. The writer had said:

Where the ancient Greeks made a distinction between the **Idiot** *as one who lives for himself and the* **Tribesman** *as one whose vision and mission is never beyond the good of the tribe and finally the* **Citizen** *as one who has a sense of the common good and therefore could truly constitute society, Nigerian leaders managed only to oscillate between idiocy and tribalism, never aspiring towards citizenship which consciously downplays self-centeredness and clannishness for a broader vision of humanity and society. Little wonder then that Fukuyama the political scientist lamented that the Nigerian State had no moral compass nor technical capacity to deliver development to citizens from a dispassionate and objective manner...*

Despite the opportunities given his country by nature, the rulers had only succeeded in turning collective wealth into fiefdoms where they flaunted their stolen assets and expected their subjects to bow and tremble at their mere sight. It remained indeed a challenge to evolve a State where resources were distributed based on need and where living in dignity was seen as the right of every citizen. As long as there were no walls around the country Nigerians would always find their way to drown at sea or scorch in the desert, and even if there were walls, the greasy palms of the officials would make a way for anyone. Therefore, there would never be a virtuous circle. Someone once asked him why Nigerians couldn't rise as one and confront the leaders and he did not hesitate in giving an answer. Everything in Nigeria was seen from a religious, regional, tribal perspective! If an Ibori was seen as corrupt by the world, he was a celebrity in the Niger Delta and if an Abacha was seen as a dictator and a looter, he was a savior in the North West. Killer herdsmen could rampage villages at night and kill helpless pregnant women, and the northern establishment would never see beyond it being a Farmer/Herders clash even when there was no aggression on the part of the now-dead; IPOB could be seen as freedom fighters by the world but perceived as worse than Boko Haram terrorists by the Northern establishment even if they had never killed a single soul. A single objective narrative was not just possible in Nigeria. So, frustrated citizens became liquefied and like water, found every single route to flow out of the country. And the tragedy was that while smaller African countries were getting it right gradually, Nigeria the big buffoon was held down by religious and regional hegemonies that sought only after the interests of their corrupt elite.

6.

Three weeks after submitting the application he got a call from his colleague in Lagos. The Catholic Church had a unit which dealt with embassies with regard to visas for its clergy and religious and the office was located in Lagos as most consular offices were. The Italian Embassy wanted him to appear in person for an interview. It was strange. For more than the eight years of going to Rome, beginning with when they would issue a visa every three months to when he began having one-year Schengen visas he had never been asked to appear for an interview! What could have gone wrong? Perhaps there was a detail he missed out or an inconsistency which needed clarification? Like two years earlier, after doing drop box at the American Embassy, he was surprisingly invited for interview only to be told that whereas in their records he had traveled to the US up to five times the previous year alone, he only indicated in the application that he traveled once. He was amazed that that was why he was being invited to appear. He apologized and said he misunderstood the question and thought all that was required was to know whether he ever visited the US previously. He was only lucky that the particular visa officer was a kind man and accepted his explanation otherwise he had the right to give him a rejection even if he had visited the US one hundred times. Actually, what happened was that the person that helped with the form advised that it didn't matter indicating all the times one had visited so long as one would write a particular instance. So maybe this invitation was about such an inconsistency?

His appointment was for 11 am so he took the early morning flight at the Nnamdi Azikiwe Airport. Luckily the AirPeace flight was right on schedule. AirPeace was one of the local airlines that was doing its best flying against the wind of heavy taxation and official bottlenecks that gave the competition to foreign African airlines. He got to Lagos by 8.05am and immediately boarded the waiting cab to the Island. It wasn't a good time for traffic but surprisingly the image he always had of Lagos as the center of chaos and gridlock disappointed slightly. Apparently, the Governor was consolidating on the work done by predecessors. Lagos was like gathering sand from the beach with a pay loader; by the time you came back the next morning the sea had washed more sand onto the beach. Yet it was possible that with deep thinking, Lagos could shed its *agbada* of befuddlement and become a city with a direction.

7.

He arrived 12 Walter Carrington Crescent, Victoria Island, exactly two and a half hours later and had to wait around for about twenty minutes before making his way to the entrance.

He was kept in a small coffee room and asked to wait for a few minutes. The Consul himself was going to see him, he was told. Suddenly he started being anxious. What was it really about that the Consul-General himself was to interview him? Quickly he scanned his application form in his mind's eye and tried to see if there was anything he had said differently in a previous application. What many Nigerian visa applicants did not know was that consistency was the official truth here. Whatever information one had first given needed to remain the truth and whatever was previously documented in any embassy could be accessed by another. People had rejections in their UK visa applications and went to lie at a Schengen visa application that they had never had a rejection, only for the fact to be pulled out and a ban placed on them for years. If you had gone to prison previously or were convicted for a drug offense overseas you simply said so because it would be discovered eventually anyway.

It was over thirty minutes and no one had come to see him. He was getting a bit agitated but decided to calm down. After all he had not scheduled any other appointment. Western Embassies made travel to their nations so difficult, and then they would turn round to blame the youths for using extra legitimate means to try to reach those places western media had painted as super heavens. Their poorest citizens could visit any part of Africa and no one dared ask whether or not they would return home but even well to do young Nigerian men and women were insulted every day at the embassies after paying humungous amounts for visas, with accusations that they would never return from the super heavens. Visas were the most sustainable scams by western nations against Nigerian youths, collecting their monies, knowing they were poor and desperate, knowing they wouldn't issue them visas, and yet still collecting without any hope of a refund. Embassies were business centers.

He took out his rosary and began to recite it. As a young priest he had found the rosary boring in its monotony. Now he was so used to it that he didn't know any other better way to pray. A prayer that took care of your present circumstances as a liable human being as well as your hour of demise had no comparison really.

He didn't know how long it took because he was carried away but suddenly the door opened and a young lady of about thirty opened the door quietly and asked if he needed a coffee or tea, apologizing over the situation, the Consul-General was held up unexpectedly. She had the prettiest eyes he had seen in a long while and with her sleeveless dress displayed the most freckle-less skin he had ever seen of any white person in the continent. She looked as if she had never been under the sun.

He preferred tea. He loved coffee but it didn't love him, it made him nervous. She was back in an instant but had to go back to get milk and sugar and sat with him making small talk. She asked him why he became a priest, what his challenges were, what his future plans were, whether he hoped someday to be a Bishop and he shook his head and said. "I want to be Pope," and they had a good laugh.

"But then you wouldn't be the first African you know. But perhaps the first black."

"That's partly true," he said. "Nowadays we are completely sold to the narrative that North Africans have always been light skinned. St. Augustine, one of the greatest theologians was black, those earlier African Popes were black, before the Moors came and conquered those territories…"

"That is true. I almost forgot. You rewrite the history then when you become Pope."

"Who knows. In the early church some people went from being lay persons straight to becoming Pope by popular acclamation. People whose lives were exemplary and saintly were sometimes acclaimed, and believe it or not they were prevailed upon, ordained, consecrated Bishop, and elected Pope. But in case you think it's a serious ambition of mine, one of the things I find depressing is the fact that you are there trying to do your best and someone else is there reading through you and thinking you have an ambition to be something else. It's annoying."

"Something else like what?"

"Like what you just asked me, like being bishop."

"Oh," she said with a little colour to her face.

"Don't misunderstand me. I mean you asked a seemingly innocent question so it's not about you. But this is the scenario. You serve in a parish or diocesan or national commission and you put in your best and people are not seeing the effort for what it is, they are sniffing around for some ambition they believe is lurking behind your whole-hearted commitment. It is sickening, whereas you don't desire to be anything other than what you are already. So, when anyone insinuates about you being bishop you just go straight for the highest office. 'No, I want to be the Pope'. But don't worry," he said with a wave of the hand. "You won't understand…By the way where did you learn your English and why are you so white?" He asked changing the subject. "You don't have that Italian accent. You speak like an American."

"I suppose it's a compliment?"

"Not really. I enjoy the musical ring around their spoken English. It is sexy."

"So, mine is boring."

"Exactly," he said. "Don't mind me. Just pulling your legs. So, let's hear how your English is so un-Italian and why you are so white."

"My parents moved to the US quite early in my life but refused to be citizens. Somehow, I too didn't see the need. I first got employed by the Italian Embassy in the US as an intern after college but I left and did a Master's before returning to the job."

"So what did you specialize in ?"

"Clinical Psychology."

He nearly spilt his drink as it dawned on him. All this while he had been under observation! These people! He remembered the promise he made to the immigration's policewoman at Fiumicino. So, she really went ahead to write a report to their embassy in Nigeria to examine him thoroughly in case he required another visa!

"I think I can guess what this is all about," he said smiling. "I smell a rat."

"We don't have rats here," she said smiling.

"We all have our down moments but it does not mean we remain low," he said. He went on to tell her about how he lost his mum and the guilt he carried for months until that healing encounter he had in Rome with a participant from Egypt. He could see her become quite calm, radiating a genuine sense of empathy. Italians loved their mothers! "But I tell you what. I am really amazed and humbled. Perhaps this is why your nations are far ahead and we Africans are always like toddlers struggling to strike a balance. You take nothing for granted while we take whole hordes for granted. I mean look at the shame on the seas and in the desert and nothing fundamental is being done by our governments… But here you are following up a harmless case. So, what's the verdict?" He asked smiling.

She excused herself and came back in fifteen minutes. "You'll have to wait for another hour and a half for the visa. Or you return tomorrow. "

"So I'm not crazy. Right ?" he asked with a veiled sneer.

"Yes you are," she said laughing. "Are you waiting or coming back tomorrow ?"

"I could do lunch and come back. Or are you inviting me to your canteen ? I love Italian food. I will pay," he quickly added.

"Of course, you will. No free lunch here. This way," she said, holding the door open. "Will take you there."

"Can I invite you sometime or its against your ethics?"

"What do you think?"

"Well, I suppose this was all part of your job but now unfortunately I like you and would want to meet you again over coffee or a meal."

"You are asking me out?" she said, raising an eyebrow and her eyes like a floodlight. That wasn't his intention and so he was a bit flustered though did his best not to show it. He had read that women admired it when a man was bold.

"Yes I am."

"And you a celibate priest asking a lady out…"

"For coffee or a meal. What's wrong with that?"

"Hmmm. The Pope must hear this."

She didn't seem to take offence as she gave him her card and circled her mobile number. He knew somehow that they had bonded and he knew just where to draw the line. A woman could be friendly but that didn't mean she wanted anything more and especially from someone who already was a liability. Many men misinterpreted the friendliness of a woman to their peril. Perhaps she really needed a friend, someone she could talk to or just hang out with. And she knew he didn't live in Lagos. Whatever the case, he had come in as a suspect and was going back with a prospect. Friendship wasn't something to shy away from, it was something which unfolding could be streamlined if it threatened to veer off the course.

BOOK FOUR

BULLETPROOF GRACE

1.

We landed safely at Heathrow.

I was getting ready to take the connecting flight to Frankfurt. I had an appointment to speak in Cologne to a group of people who wanted to hear firsthand, my experiences in the hands of kidnappers. A string of priests had been kidnapped by the dreaded Fulani herdsmen and I had become one of their unfortunate victims. A colleague who had volunteered with us for two years back in Nigeria and returned to Germany heard about my ordeal and got some friends together so they could listen to me and raise some support for my proposed initiative called *Sane Rainforests*. It was an advocacy initiative in which we were going to draw the attention of government and the international community to the communities of the rainforests especially in terms of their infrastructure. The fundraising was for Mkpot, a community tucked in the middle of the forest. It was one of the last initiatives I was promoting before leaving my position as country director and taking up a pastoral assignment.

With the whole concern about climate change and how these forests contribute oxygen to the ecosystem, these communities needed to be 'spoilt silly'. But here they were, completely neglected, while government collected huge revenue from the pool of carbon taxes and sat on international forestry boards. The communities were prevented by law from exploiting forest resources and yet government had not been able to provide them with alternatives. The worst part was that there wasn't a good passable road! These communities cultivated banana, plantain, cocoa, cocoyam, cassava, and these produces were left to rot because of poor evacuation due to poor roads. Successive administrations in the state had paid little attention to people of these communities because they didn't have prominent indigenes who spoke on their behalf. We wanted to have an international advocacy for the area because Nigerian politicians listened better to foreigners. If you said something in Nigeria, no matter how important, if you didn't follow it up with a violent threat or action, no one took you seriously. The other way was to go abroad and have people overseas advocating for a local issue and then you would have the attention of government. This is what I was going to do in Cologne. But first let me tell you about the kidnap!

2.

That fateful day, we had embarked on a mapping exercise of the bad spots on the major road that led through the Oban corridor of the rain forest. The other flank of the rain forest is in Boki area of the state. The road led from Calabar to Ekang. Despite the hype that greeted the approval of the contract by the 7th Senate for the reconstruction of the Trunk A federal road since it was first done by Costain West

Africa in 1972, nothing much was done after several billions had been paid to the contractor. In a terrible twist of fate, the Chinese construction company had instead gone to the best part of the road and excavated it and sold off the scraps and then abandoned the project. When we enquired as to why it was the good portion of the road that was destroyed, we were asked to thank our stars as the company didn't excavate beyond the bridge because normally according to practice, as the first part of the contract, they should excavate the entire road!

This Chinese company used Nigerian peoples' money, turned the best part of the road into a nightmare for motorists and walked away with billions of naira as having completed the first part of the project! I had long known that contracts were not awarded for the common good but this particular case beat my entire imagination. I couldn't understand how something that was meant to make something better rather made it impossible. Instead of using the amount that was allocated that year for the rehabilitation of the worst sections of the road, they took the easiest option of excavating the best part that was closest to the city so they and their backers could divide the money knowing full well that additional funds may not be forthcoming and that the road would be abandoned in a more terrible state!

We wanted to get the true state of the road complete with pictures and coordinates so that we could do some advocacy with the Federal Ministry of Works and the Federal Ministry of Environment, along with multi-lateral institutions such as the World Bank.

That day we got to the border alright after identifying about 27 terrible stretches. These were no more pot holes. Long burrows had emerged on the road that stretched sometimes for more than a kilometer, with mounds of dried mud walls on both sides. It was passable because it was the dry season. During the rains, these mud melted and became thick rivers of clay porridge and made the roads impassable except for four wheel drives and farm tractors. Farm produce became bad because it could not be evacuated and those who had any business in the city had to pay through their noses for the sixty kilometer journey that would now take five hours to make.

It was more annoying when we walked across the bridge into Cameroonian territory and saw that they were reconstructing their roads. Cameroon that had a reputation for bad roads especially in the English-speaking territories were rehabilitating their roads! The immigration officials explained to us that because of the African Championships the government had embarked on rehabilitating the roads to enhance free flow of traffic all over the country! It was distressing that in spite of all the tourism potential Nigeria had, there was no national strategy to tie infrastructure development to tourism. I was furious as I took out my notebook to copy out the coordinates and send as an email to myself and Zel my friend. Although there was no GSM signal along these communities, the mails would deliver as soon as my browser detected a GSM signal as I was using Outlook.

It was during the return leg shortly after we saw a tank stand with solar panels in one village and stopped out of curiosity that it happened. We were quite excited as we made to find out if the water project was functioning. Alas! It was the Border Commission that installed the tank with solar panels and laid pipes to reticulate water to various points in the community but without digging any borehole for water or establishing any water works. I was sure they had already reported on the project as done! It was shortly after inspecting the water project and driving off to the next major bad stretch of caked muddy burrows that the kidnappers struck.

3.

"Jeez!" our driver screamed.

I looked up and saw them. Two tall lanky youths with slightly curled hair standing in the middle of the road one wielding a stick and flagging us down and the other wielding a sub machine gun and pointing it at us! My hands and legs began to tremble, I felt a sudden rush in my bowels and I started panting as my heartbeat accelerated. We slowed down.

"Father drive through and crush them," Husseini the driver said.

"What!"

"Just drive through, all we do is lie low so that even if they shoot the bullets won't get to us."

"We won't try anything funny," I said. Though I wasn't coordinated I could still remember the admonition that we should never resist an armed man. In the midst of the frenzy and the dissonance of thoughts in my head, one thing was certain, we were being kidnapped.

Now I understood why I had taken over the wheels from him after we inspected the solar tank. I myself was surprised when I told him I needed to drive a bit. I was sure that if he was still the one behind the wheels he would have tried something funny. The unfortunate thing was that because of the terrible condition of the road there was no other vehicle along the road as most vehicles either stopped at Oban or Osomba village if they ever went far.

We stopped the car. I was dressed very casually with jeans and Tee shirt and since I was driving they thought the driver was the boss, as he was a bit on the heavy side, with a slightly protruding belly. The one with the stick banged it on the car bonnet and ordered us to come down while the one with the gun still held it this time pointing at the driver. They searched our pockets and took the money we had. Then the car was searched and they recovered my phone, an I-Phone.

"Na who getam for dis phone?" the one with the stick asked.

"Na me."

"How I be driba ni ? " He was asking how come I was the driver and with such a phone. My phone was the latest iPhone. Apparently, they knew all makes of phones.

"Na me be oga," I said. "Leave am for me ni. Carry me ni." I gesticulated, pointing to myself as the boss. Husseini had a wife and kids and I had none. I was celibate. It was better I be taken than him. Then Husseini turned into Hausa. I didn't understand what he was saying. "Me na oga ko." I said again. I was just trying to speak pidgin English the way uneducated Hausa-Fulani peasants spoke it for obviously they were the famous herdsmen.

Herdsmen had almost become invincible and omnipresent. They were all over the nation's forests and especially our rainforests. They understood the terrain better than the natives. They used to be simple peasants who needed only fodder for their pasture.

But from simple stick bearing cattle-herds, they turned into machine gun wielding human-herds for they now dealt with a kind of animal that would not be herded by a mere stick. It all began because of cattle rustling. As most herdsmen made the forests their abode it became an increasing occurrence that strong herdsmen would rustle the cattle of weaker cousins. As the Nigerian state had not finished securing the lives of people that lived in towns and villages, it was impossible to police the forests. Many herders' families resorted to self-help. They began establishing a tradition of training the male child on how to handle the machine gun. Each lead herder was thus equipped with a gun so he could confront rustlers. As guns became a tradition and rustling reduced, the criminal elements found a new outlet. Kidnapping became a multi-billion naira business overnight when Boko Haram fighters joined the fray as a means of fundraising for their campaigns. As banks in Nigeria mainstreamed the cashless policy and internet banking became fully operationalized burglaries and armed robberies for cash reduced drastically as people no longer stashed cash at home. Ransom became the new return- on-investment as kidnap victims' families would rally round to raise funds to pay. In the cities down south of Nigeria kidnaps were done by cult boys and ex-militants. But if you were kidnapped in the middle of nowhere and taken into a forest, it was likely going to be by a Fulani herdsman. I had read about many kidnap incidents especially through WhatsApp groups. Many clerics had been kidnapped, some even killed. I never knew I could be a victim, in my very native soil!

"I dey joke am for me bah?" He was asking whether

I was joking with him, and raised the stick to hit me on the head but Husseini pleaded again in Hausa. Somehow, I noticed that the Hausa Husseini spoke with them had softened them. Husseini now spoke in pidgin so I could hear too.

"Let my driba (driver) go for arrange ransom ni?" Husseini said and turned again to Hausa. I now understood what he was trying to do. He didn't want me kidnapped thinking it was probably better I left so I could quicken his release than me to be taken but I thought better. I now turned to Husseini to play along. "Oga let me go with them. Stay back oga." At this point I felt a loud and painful smack on my back. I fell down writhing in pain. He hit me again and ordered me to get up. "I dey joke am for me? I dey joke am for me?" And hit me again. "Oya standam por up. Go." He was angry that I appeared to be thinking he was joking.

Apparently the one with the stick was the boss. He led the way into the forest ordering both of us to follow while the one with the gun came from behind. My back ached as we trekked deep into the forest. I lost count of the hours. Our feet were rising and falling in painful rhythm. They had taken away our wrist watches but did not take our wrist bands. I was very hungry and thirsty and was almost fainting from the pain and hunger, as I noticed that it was becoming dark.

I had lived a very simple and protected life without hassles for as long as I could remember. I did not engage in strenuous exercises nor work-outs so my body was not ready for this at all. I started breathing very heavily and slumped. They allowed us rest for a while. Husseini was exhausted too but obviously he was stronger. He was speaking to them in Hausa. They allowed us to rest seeing that I couldn't continue.

In the middle of the forest one thing I was grateful for was that they had not taken off the wristband I wore on my left hand. I had great hope that something good would happen. You see several months earlier, because we read about the kidnap of an NGO team in Benue, our IT team designed a tracking system for staff who go into the field. There was a device in the car that the driver had to activate if there was suspicion of a carjack. Field staff were required to wear a wristband that had a chip embedded in one of the beads that one had to press to activate. The device was configured to send an SMS and an email simultaneously to a number and an address already configured after which it would start reporting the staff's location intermittently to an online dashboard which could also be monitored on a cellphone by the security manager. It would then be the security manager's responsibility to keep track of location and work with law enforcement. While the herdsmen thought nobody knew about our location, probably by this time, there was already a frenzy. If it were overseas we would have been rescued within the hour because we had done our own bit by being proactive. But in Nigeria, the response time to issues was the main reason criminality thrived. By the time law enforcement got their act together, the criminals would have completed their tasks and gone far. Some people actually believed that criminals worked in concert with law enforcement, that was why it was only on rare cases that the response time was good. Besides I had to be realistic; while overseas, law enforcement had access to all kinds of equipment even helicopters, Nigeria law enforcement often had no money to fuel their beaten down vehicles. If you wanted your case to be fast tracked, you had to furnish the police with necessary 'logistics'. Long ago I had concluded that in Nigeria the reality was crime and *furnishment* because while truly in other nations a crime was against the state and the state could spend millions of dollars to get to the root of a case, in Nigeria a crime in reality was against the victim and the victim often had to furnish the police with the cost if he or she wanted justice and because many couldn't bear the unproductive cycles of exploitation they let go of many matters.

4.

Have you ever felt like giving up? Like dying? Well, that is how I Fr Itanja felt. I realized that death was coming very fast, that death is life's sibling. Every other thing didn't matter to me as the thought of the hereafter. It was amazing when we strived so much in life only to confront the truth that nothing really matters more than life itself and we should be daily grateful for a day that we have spent doing our own thing in peace. To be free was a great thing, to be alive and free was the greatest thing.

"Oya. Stan ap," the stick bearing one said and hit me again. I stood up. We continued walking until darkness fell completely and they brought out a torchlight from their bag and began to lead the way with it. I was grateful to God that it was the dry season. What if it was during the rains?

My feet could not carry me any longer and I fell again. I was tired, hungry, thirsty, dying. Husseini was begging them to allow us rest again. I sat leaning on a tree trunk and dozed off. Luckily, I had half of a piece of bitter kola in my pocket and even as I was tempted to take it out and chew because of hunger, I was afraid they might suspect my movement if I tried to take it from my pocket, so now it would act as a repellant against snakes. We had grown up to know that snakes were repelled by the smell of bitter kola.

I don't know how long I slept. I don't know how many lions or Chimps came our way and passed by or how many antelopes galloped past our company in that dead of night because I was fast asleep. It was humbling to realize that sometimes the greatest need you could have in the entire multiples of galaxies was just to be allowed an hour of sleep. I couldn't even remember the dream I had. But I slept soundly and deeply, weighed down by my tiredness and hunger. I was woken up by a thwack on my head. I stood up in a daze and tripped on a shrub and fell. I balanced up as they laughed at me.

Love your enemies… I was a preacher too and it was so easy to preach stuff like that. I tell you, the very thought of that verse was momentarily annoying. All I wanted to do now was crush their heads and get away from this horrible dream. But somehow the thought passed like a spasm. I began to whisper under my breath "Come O Holy Spirit Fill the Heart of thy Faithful…"

They didn't seem to have any compassion or interest in what happened to any of us. They didn't even seem to have any humanity. They seemed only interested in taking us to somewhere they could begin to make negotiations for ransom. Lanky, uneducated, they valued not their lives nor the lives of others. At the slightest provocation they could maim you or kill you without a thought and they would not be brought to book possibly because it was difficult to enter the forest and make an arrest. And if they were ever arrested for any crime, before you knew it high profile telephone calls would be placed by high ranking chiefs to high ranking officials of state and they would walk free. But woe betide, if any of them was found dead near your community, maybe killed as a result of a fracas which the dead man initiated; the entire community could be burnt down, the women and children raped and killed ! The governor of a state who himself was Fulani had declared that each of the herdsmen's lives were worth the lives of ten innocent ordinary men, women and children, in a sentence executed by the herdsmen themselves, often when law enforcement would be nowhere to be found. It was worse if a cow died alongside, for the cows were worth more than their lives and therefore your own life as well. If any of their cows was killed by a member of any community, human lives had to appease the dead cow. The herdsmen looked ordinary but they were no mean citizens because their tribe was a no mean tribe. People joked that apart from the governor and his deputy and the president and his vice who had immunity de jure and de facto others that had immunity de facto were the herdsmen.

5.

It was the early hours of dawn. We were given marching orders to continue the movement but I told them I wanted to pray. Surprisingly they stepped back and allowed us. I called Husseini forward and we knelt down and held hands and prayed, thanking God for life and asking for strength and his divine intervention. We even sang a few choruses and then I gave the blessing. I asked God to forgive the herdsmen and bless them and keep them alive to see their wives and children and members of their families.

The movement continued.

Then we came upon a brook. I shouted spontaneously "Alleluia." The herder turned and smacked me on the back for shouting.

"Allah forgive you." I said to him mustering all my strength. "Why do you beat me for praising God? God will not be happy with you," I said, filled with a sudden rage and without a care anymore whether I would be alive or dead. "What will you gain by all this wickedness of yours? You can never enter paradise unless you repent. You are an unbeliever." Then I said the only Hausa I knew. "Dan banza."

Suddenly he went mad with rage, grabbed the gun from his colleague, cocked it and shouted "Allahu Akbr," and fired. I had closed my eyes, whispering under my breath. "Lord Jesus receive my spirit," surprisingly with no iota of fear. I did not brave up so he could kill me but there are moments you should cease claim to your very humanity if you could not project your voice; if this would lead to my death so be it, I wouldn't be the first nor the last to die in the forest.

I opened my eyes when I noticed that it was taking too long. By this time Husseini was crying and on bended knees begging in Hausa but he seemed quite adamant as he struggled with the gun. I watched as he directed it at me again and pressed the trigger and nothing happened. Then he pointed it skywards and there was a loud bang which caused birds to fly out of their nests and sudden movement in the forest as certain animals apparently ran helter-skelter. He directed it at me again and nothing happened. At this point I knew God had sent his angels to intervene. A sudden strength filled me up. He fired on one of the nearby trees and there was a bang but no bang when he directed it at me again. I saw that fear enveloped them. They had a syncretic culture of mixing up charms with their religion so they probably thought my charm was a more potent one. Or maybe they just plain knew it was God at work. My joy was that it had not occurred to them to try the gun on Husseini whom they seemed to have some rapport because he spoke Hausa with them. I loved God for confusing them for I did not know if that bulletproof grace extended to Husseini as well.

I had to act quickly.

Without their guns they were as powerless as any feeble boy. Should not we tackle them? But then I imagined that God did not begin a good work and leave it uncompleted. I should not try to take matters into my hands.

I do not know where the initiative came from. I said to them in a commanding voice. "Oya. Go. Leave us alone or you die here," using my index finger to gesticulate. They stood for a moment contemplating. "Give my phone ni," I said stretching my hand. Not surprisingly he brought the phones out. I knew God was giving me authority over them. "Oya. Go away." I said again, half afraid, sounding as if I would harm them if they did not move immediately. They left us hurriedly. The gun wielding one saying something in Hausa to Husseini. He turned to me. "They want to drink and fetch water." I nodded an okay but asked Husseini to tell them to hurry up. Quickly they drank some water, fetched some, crossed the brook and disappeared.

The forest was vast but my elementary geography told me to follow the trail of the stream. If we trailed it downwards it might lead us deeper into the forest so we decided to go upstream. We did not also discountenance the fact that the herdsmen could be hiding somewhere watching us. We walked by the bank of the stream upwards for about two hours until we got to where the water had collected into a kind of pool. Having been brought up in a village, I knew there must be a neighboring village that used this stream as its source of water more so because I thought I saw a well beaten footpath.

By this time, I was already feeling sick because of my breath. I wasn't sure if this was the section they fetched to drink because many communities cordoned off sections of the stream to bath leaving a lower section for women and an upper section for men but I needed to wash up and rinse my mouth. No sooner had I pulled off than we saw two teenagers coming to fetch water. They ran off shouting that men had come to bath in the female section. I used the native tongue to call them back, telling them we were lost and needed help. They seemed to believe us as they took our advice to wait for us to accompany them to the village. I wore my clothes again and washed my face and rinsed my mouth with the water. I was not afraid because it was a flowing stream and under the circumstances there was nothing else I could do. I told them we would wait for them if they wanted to bath and fetch water.

I was surprised when they told me the name of the community was Mkpot. Now if you know Mkpot, it had no access road, you had to trek for about 24 kilometers from Ntebachot junction where the international road was. Only a motor bike could manage parts of the way during the dry season. The community had relocated twice and yet went back to resettle in its original abode. When Oban Hills Forest was gazetted in 1933 they became part of the gazetted area as government did not carve out the community. When the Cross River National Park Decree 36 of 1991 was enacted, the people were asked to relocate but with no alternative provided typical of the way government handled matters. The people refused. However, it was a rustic community in the middle of the forest without good drinking water or electricity. The Catholic Archbishop who had visited the community thrice was spearheading advocacy for the community and it was through him I already knew a lot about the community. Since I had already known that their streams dried up during the dry season and they had to go far into the forest to fetch water, I knew we were in for another long trek.

Well. It wasn't so bad, as we trekked for about eight kilometers, because we walked for about one hour forty minutes, using an average of 12.5 minutes per kilometer. It was really excruciating, walking that kind of distance just to fetch water.

The village was thrown into turmoil when we arrived. Apparently news of our kidnap had spread everywhere by now. Many of them had heard of my name, the elderly ones even knew my parents and had attended my ordination years ago and many of the women and youths were seeing me for the first time.

They were openly weeping and praising God. It was so emotional that I broke down too and began to weep for this community tucked away in the forest and yet no government had considered it worthwhile to give them even an access road. I wept for the stagnant pools of water and the possible mosquito infestations. I wept for the lack of health or educational facility. I wept for their joy which was so infectious. Finally, the little crowd led us to the *Ntufam's* palace who was so kind as to welcome us and give us a meal.

I was anxious to know what was happening in the outside world. I asked if they had GSM signal and I was told a young man had a contraption with a cable which he tied to a long pole and connected the wire ends to his phone for signals. He offered to make a call on our behalf for free. I switched on my phone, as I had switched it off to save the battery. I scrolled to the security manager's number and attempted to dial with my phone but there was no signal. I was told there was an elevated spot I could get signal from but it was a bit far. I declined. I gave him the number to dial. I think at this point everyone was waiting to hear from the kidnappers what their terms were because he literally picked the call at the first ring and answered quite anxiously "Hello?"

"Uche. It's me."

"Father !!!" he screamed. He said something to me that sounded plain but which was a code to know whether I was under duress or not. "I am safe," I told him, cutting off the security protocols. I asked him to call the number instead so I don't deplete the young man's top-up. "So, what's been happening? It's been more than twenty-four hours and nothing from the security agencies?" I asked when he called back.

He began to explain how the police said they had contacted the Commissioner of Police in the state and how they had requested for money to use their own tracking system to interpret the location, and how they had been given five hundred thousand naira to cover five days and the police was saying that since it seemed to be in the middle of the forest they would have to wait until we advanced close to a major road. So, they had been waiting anxiously tracking our movement. They had informed the police when they noticed we were in that village and that they were getting ready to mobilize and come to the community with about five bikes. They had given the police money to hire a truck that would carry the bikes to a point where they could use them, they would then get locals along the way to lead them. I asked him to tell them that we were safe now although the idea of bikes was a good one. I was afraid that typical of Nigerian police, they could come and arrest the innocent villagers and take them to the city, and then their families would come and bail them out with huge sums of money. I had an eternal dread of policemen in my country because they were trained to turn any misdemeanor into a crime. And there was no alibi in their dictionaries. No matter how foolproof your case was, no matter how excellent your alibi was, you had to visit the station, make a statement, be detained and then bailed with money.

He told me that the vehicle had been immobilized by the insurance company already so there was no fear of it being stolen except someone removed the tires. I asked him to call the insurance company to activate it again as we might have to go to get it. Luck was on us that day as a young man who owned a bike in that village had fallen sick that morning and couldn't take any passengers on the 24-kilometer ride to the major road but recuperated with the excitement in the village. We begged the *Ntufam* to allow us to leave and promised him that we would not forget his community, that God had a reason for making us have an appearance there.

6.

That is how we left the village, the Ntufam having paid for us. I prayed for the community and blessed them.

The bike ride was the best we could get. At some points we would disembark and push the bike up the hill, as the community seemed to be in a valley. At other times the terrain was too rough for passengers so we walked along. But finally, we got to the main road and while I rested in Ntebachot village, to another uproar, he took Husseini to bring the car hoping that the insurance company had mobilized it already.

About two hours later, Husseini came back with the car and we did not waste time setting out on the journey home. Twenty minutes later we saw a beaten down police truck just before Akor Village and we stopped. The van had broken down. The truck had four bikes and six policemen. I suspected they were the ones sent to rescue us. They affirmed my suspicion. I told them we were the victims and we were alright. I asked what was wrong with their vehicle and they told me they had run out of fuel, as the vehicle's carburetor was not functioning properly and consumed a lot of fuel. I did not want to tell them I had been informed they charged money to hire a truck. They insisted I take pictures with them, and they all posed around us with their rifles. Husseini helped a few to take pictures and a short video. Two of the policemen insisted on accompanying us in our own vehicle as security detail. Well the back seat was empty. But they insisted I move to the chauffeur driven side while two of them sat in front. I asked one of them to join me behind.

As soon as we came into GSM network area, the one behind put a call through to someone. I heard him say. "We have him sir." I turned and looked at him and he whispered "Commissioner." He kept saying "Yes sir. Yes sir," to whatever. He handed me the phone and said "Commissioner wants to speak with you." The commissioner of police was so nice and apologetic, saying they did all they could in the circumstances and asked that I pass by his office as soon as we got to Calabar. He would not take no for an answer and promised he just wanted to set his eyes on me, that was all, that I must be a very important person for the Inspector General himself to have called him.

Well, I passed straight to his office as soon as we arrived Calabar, although to my surprise there was a video camera that filmed me as I stepped down from the vehicle with the policemen and as the commissioner of police himself welcomed me into his office. True to his promise he did not keep me for long. I thanked him for sending his men, although we had already found our way out. He asked me to pray for Nigeria so that those in authority take the funding of the police more seriously. I said to him that while we wait for the big break that he should always do what was within his power and do it excellently well; that if all the police commands could do their best with the little they had, we would go a long way in fighting crime.

7.

I did not really understand what was happening with the police until I saw the news later that evening. It was on several networks, I was told. There was a footage of me as I arrived the station in the company of two policemen, a flash of the picture we took with the policemen when we met them along the road, my meeting with the commissioner, and his seeing me off. The commissioner was quoted as saying that the Nigeria Police would continue to do everything within its powers to protect the lives of citizens, and he was happy to announce that he had successfully put together a crack team of policemen to rescue me close to Mkpot, a community 24 kilometers inside the forest.

I had come back to realize that the news of the kidnap was all over the social media especially twitter and Facebook; being a leader of a national organization with international affiliation, the news had also gone round 169 countries. The footage of the commissioner announcing the rescue, was picked up as well and spread on social media, with many people praising the uncommon effort of the Nigerian police, as the kidnap had lasted less than 48 hours.

I did not say anything to the contrary. Aljazeera got back to speak to me. I told them it was a combination of divine assistance and human intelligence. I said our office was able to link with the police who kept track of our location every hour. When they asked me if the police actually rescued me, I deflected the question by asking them if they were suggesting that the police commissioner was lying. Going through the commissioner's statement again, I saw that he only said the police put together a crack team to rescue us and stopped short of saying they actually rescued us. I had nothing to debunk. There was so much bad news that if they made effort to do something good, I would only commend that effort.

So, that is how we decided to create a campaign to support rainforest communities, focusing first on this community that had been my first contact with decent humanity again. My friends in Cologne wanted to hear the story from the horse's mouth, as they say.

<h2 style="text-align:center">8.</h2>

Now back to Heathrow, it was my turn to do the security check.

As soon as I crossed over I would go and have a cup of coffee and a croissant. I was already hungry and I had about two hours to wait before my next flight. My plan was that after the event in Cologne, I would visit Aachen for a day and return to Frankfurt to take an evening flight back to the UK, this time through Gatwick. I planned to then spend about two weeks with a priest colleague of mine in High Wycombe.

I did not have any luggage checked in, just a laptop bag and a carry-on bag. Ever since I lost my luggage for nearly a month in Air France, and another incident that made me skip an important function because I spent four days waiting for my missing luggage from Lufthansa, I decided that no matter how long the trip was going to last, my things would have to fit into a carry-on bag.

It didn't matter that I came with British Airways from Abuja and hadn't left the airport, I would still have to do a security check to board the next plane!

I pulled out a tray and pulled off my jacket and dropped it inside. I removed my belt too. My phone was in my jacket. I first passed my carry-on bag. I took out my lap top and iPad, put them on a separate tray and passed across the body scanner safely to the other side and waited for my bags to arrive.

Suddenly I encountered what could be the worst fears of anyone: being thought of as a terrorist! The conveyor belt stopped, giving off a very loud beep.

"Did you pack this bag yourself?"

"Yes. It's my travel bag. I arrived with British Airways this morning. I haven't left the airport. I am going to Frankfurt."

"Okay. But do you know the exact content of the bag?"

"Of course, I do. It's a bag I travel all the time with. It's my lap top bag."

She checked the scanner again turning the image over and over.

"I'm afraid I am going to get my supervisor." I shrugged. She could go call the Mayor himself. Shortly afterwards a man came forward to question me.

"Do you have any device with batteries inside the bag?"

"Device with batteries…" I tried to recall, confused. "Not so sure."

"So you don't know the content of the bag then."

"I do. It's my bag. "

"Then what do you have inside the bag that is radioactive?" I was speechless, totally at a loss.

"Truly I can't say. Why not take out the bag and examine it?"

"I can't do that. We can't risk it. There might be an explosion."

"Explosion!" I shouted inadvertently.

"I am sorry I will have to call the Police." Police!

They cleared other passengers from that section of the security hall. I wasn't shaken because I knew my bag had been with me all the time and I was quite sure there was no strange content after all I had passed it through the scanners at the airport in Abuja before embarkation.

"You see, I am a ... Oh I do remember. Could be my computer mouse, the batteries from my lap top mouse," I called out to him.

"I am sorry. The bomb squad will be here any minute. They will find out by themselves."

I waited calmly.

Five minutes later a swath of Police officers, about nine of them, wearing bomb proof vests and carrying what was obviously a bomb disposal equipment appeared. My heart began to beat a little faster as the bag was brought out. One of the policemen stood by chatting with me probably in a bid to ease my tension.

"I have a story to tell my parishioners when I get home," I said to him with a confident smile.

"Let's hope it goes well," he responded. *Let's hope it goes well?* Suddenly I was struck with panic. Suppose I was really in trouble! After I had successfully evaded being kidnapped for a ransom suppose someone had actually planted a device in my bag because there were professionals who would do that without your knowing. Suppose there was media waiting and my image would be broadcast all over the world for something I knew nothing about? Suppose I would head here straight to detention and then to court and prison, what would I say? Years ago, being who I was would have been credible enough to let me go but over time my stock had given enough scandal to the world to doubt our best intentions. Would I, a priest of God come and add terrorism to it?

I was innocent. "God knows I am innocent" I began to say to myself. "We'll see."

We'll see ? Oh my. They really believed I was carrying an explosive device!

After a few tense moments, there it was, a set of old batteries in a broken laptop mouse! I heaved a sigh of relief. They scanned the bag again but the beeping continued.

At this point I became totally confused. Could someone have inserted something while the bag was in the overhead locker while in midair? I hardly fell asleep while flying otherwise I would say someone took the bag while I fell asleep. I had not checked in the bag so I couldn't even imagine the possibility of someone loading any strange matter in it while in storage. What could have happened between coming out of one plane, window shopping, and preparing to board another plane?

My mind went everywhere.

Finally, it was something quite unexpected that ended the beeping. A tablet of Dettol Soap! I had bought it and thrown it into my laptop bag because in many of the hotels I was booked in, they didn't have antiseptic soaps and I developed rashes if I didn't use antiseptic soaps. I had failed to put it into the transparent plastic bag provided at the security point. There must be something about its packaging that emitted rays akin to radioactive ones.

"Hmmm" I sighed.

Everyone went away in an anticlimax. I nearly burst out laughing when I saw the embarrassment on the supervisor's face. If only he had listened to me! In my country, the mere fact of who I was would have made him listen except that traffickers, gun runners, kidnappers enjoyed same privileges although in their own case the justice hook was too thin to catch them because they were heavy on cash. But here, they had to get to the very bottom of the matter no matter who I claimed to be. In a way I was also lucky that it did not happen in my country, because the mere fact that there was suspicion would have been enough to take me away until I proved my innocence and some cash parted ways.

The incident at Heathrow would be an interesting anecdote to my presentation at Cologne. Cologne was the richest catholic Archdiocese in the world at some point. I was really hoping that even if the effort of my former colleague would not yield much, the publicity after the event would generate more goodwill. We planned to bring an expert to Mkpot to study the environment in order to advise on the best way to create access to water during the dry season for members of that community. We also wanted to train a few community members on basic health services before establishing a health post. We needed also a vector expert to sensitize the community on vector control so to avoid cases of malaria. Above all we wanted to lead advocacy to the World Bank to construct the 24-kilometer road in partnership with the Cross River State government as the Catholic Archbishop had already started by grading eight kilometers of the road.

9.

I was already back from Cologne and ready to start my leave. The event was successful as there were lots of online media attention. It was streamed live and many people tuned in. By the third day after the event, there were pledges already amounting to one hundred thousand euros. It was amazing, the generosity of the German people, and that was because pictures and short videos of the community were put online for viewing. Two water engineers had also volunteered to fly to Nigeria at their own expense but needed accommodation and local transportation. It moved me to see how people loved humanity. Not that they had enough to overflow but they were always ready to sacrifice their luxuries for the needs of the very poor. I was no expert in water resources so I did not bother thinking how it was going to work but the idea I had was to leverage the resources we would raise and request the local government for counterpart funding. The only snag was that the local government system was barely functional as the State government had appropriated all its resources through the fraudulent joint account system. I decided that I would not bother myself with all these issues during these two weeks I was going to spend with my friend in the UK. As I landed, this time, at Gatwick, I resolved that I would transfer everything I had to do back home to the waiting list until the two weeks of holidays were over.

BOOK FIVE

ONE FOOL DAY

1.

It was the third year running visiting Yakubu in High Wycombe and getting introduced to the same set of people. Ever since Yaks, as I called him, went over, it was easier for me to have a spot to spend my holiday. For many of us holiday just meant leaving your country and your schedule and going over to a friend's place in another country to join in his schedule. White people did not look so much alike as the Chinese, so I could identify faces somewhat. But names! And every year, it was the same rigmarole.

"Hello Father" Theirs was easy. They didn't even need to know my name, my title was enough.

"Hi"

"Rosa. We met last year. Remember? I gave you a lift from …"

"Oh yes. Rosa. Pardon me. How are you doing?"

I remembered her now. Since I couldn't drive, many members of the congregation gave me lifts severally. Rosa was certainly one of them. We would go on discussing the weather and all the chit chat that could get two perfect strangers talking without even caring to get introduced.

How did you really grow your attention span? How

do you make something stick? Because I have got into too much 'trouble' that I am beginning to think there is something wrong with me. I hear a name and it so fills my head that you would think it would take ages to recede. The next moment I have to ask Yaks what the name was.

Yaks was different. He knew his members all by name. "Meet Amir. This is Sally and Kuma… Oh there is Andes. Andes has a son that plays the accordion." The kids gave him high fives. Just by a casual acquaintance, Yaks could reel out the names of an entire group of twenty. Secretly I wondered if he had a photographic implant which recorded every word, every move. I was always conscious of saying things true since a lie needed another to cover up the last. Our conversations would always end like. "But you said Theodore wore an off-white dress at the occasion."

"Oh yes. She didn't?"

"And now you are saying she wore white."

It was somewhat irritating, this ease at minutiae, the comfort with detail, the appetite to be exact. Why could not people like Yaks just be satisfied that she wore a dress?

Boring.

This time I had come prepared to drive. I had come with an international driver's license. I was going to spend two weeks and I was going to make sure there was no dull moment. If it were London I wouldn't bother with the car. I loved London. There was something so equal about the city. As soon as you landed at Heathrow, there were trains that took you to every part of the country. There were coaches too. Oh, how I loved the underground. Just get the Oyster and you could ride and ride and ride. London was a city that even the rich could do without a car. Sometimes I would take the rail from High Wycombe to Marylebone, take the Booker Line and come off at Paddington, roam around Hyde Park, take Bus 24 to Oxford Circus and just feast my eyes. Here you did not even know who was rich or poor because everyone caught the bus or train. But in my native land… They allowed the trains to rot because they all got cars, and cared less about the few rickety coaches. Then they allowed the inter-State roads to grow large mouths that drank the blood of the poor because they could fly to the capital. I had concluded that a politician's rationality was a matter of faith because there was no evidence!

"I want to go to the City Centre," I announced to Yaks.

"Okay. You know the bus to take. 33. It takes you right to the station."

"I know. I want to drive."

"I beg your pardon? Did you just say you want to drive?" He stared at me for a brief moment. "You know you cannot drive in this country. You don't have a license."

"Tadaaa." I pulled my international driver's license out of my wallet. Yaks examined every detail as if his eyes could see through the embedded chip.

"Do you need a mercury light bulb?" I asked jokingly. There was no stopping me.

Yaks had two cars at his disposal. The only child of an old lady had died crushed by a vehicle at a Zebra crossing. A car had stopped for her to cross with her baby cart when another fully throttling, came from the rear and could not stop soon enough. Mother and child died hours apart. So, the old lady had donated her daughter's car. Yaks said he was going to hold consultations with the council and recommend an outright sale so the funds could be put into a trust. He hardly drove the car. But that was last year and the car was still there.

"You win. Okay. Use mine."

I collected the keys quickly and jumped into the car before he would change his mind. As I reversed to leave, he flagged me down. I wound down the window. "Remember it's the left. They drive on the left."

"I know. The steering is of course on the right so it should be easy."

"Just remember."

<h1 style="text-align:center">2.</h1>

I sped off. In fact, one of the reasons I was insistent on driving was my fascination with the left drive. I remember way back as a kid when my native land had to change from driving on the left to the right. It was always amazing arriving London and seeing vehicles go clockwise at the roundabout. I knew why Yaks was this emphatic. On one occasion I had nearly been hit trying to cross a busy road as I looked left when I should look right. I wanted to know what it would feel like driving on the left.

I had spent the first two days going over the traffic manual so I was acquainted with most details. I wouldn't dare make a mistake that would attract the attention of the police. In my native land the police could be intimidated by someone behind the wheel especially if it was a big car with dark shades on the window and back screens because you never knew if he or she was the cousin of a big politician who with one phone call to the police commissioner could send you to a less 'lucrative' spot. Or even if not so, the police understood the law was made for man and not man for the law so if your papers were expired or you committed a traffic offence all you had to do was plead for understanding and of course leave a tip behind. A bribe was before a service, a tip was after a service! And I loved all those police men. Were they really corrupt? They had never said to me, "Unless you give me a bribe you won't drive past,"; they rather always saluted you and asked "Anything for the boys?" And I would always smile and say "Next time", and they would let me go. Or I would tell them I would pray for them. It amazed me always that they believed I would actually do, so I always tried to. Everyone in my native land so always seemed to have a need for prayers that even road repairs were a prayer point.

As for these British Police, there was no messing with them. Or should I say English Police? I smiled as I remembered a chat I had with one of those grand old ladies after Mass just a day before. What was her name? Bloomington or so. Since many of them would always ask me where I came from, how long I would stay, when exactly I was leaving, I made it a point also to ask each of them where they came from originally and if they had plans to relocate from the UK! I was being mischievous but you see it was a mixed community. A lady I thought was British was actually Brazilian. She had been over in the UK for more than twenty years and lived with her grandchildren. So last week when I chatted with Bloomington she gave me that English angle.

"You are originally from the UK right?" I asked her.

"Of course. England," she answered with some flow of blood to her face showing that it was an annoying question.

"I see. It's such a mixed community so sometimes I get confused. Not that it matters though. It's amazing how Britain has a mix of all races as her citizenry," I said smiling, truly amazed at how a nation could open its doors to others who even became political leaders. A few of my countrymen were in parliament and Khan had become mayor of London.

"Britain is so accommodating," I said again, as I noticed her silence.

"Yes, she is. They become British. Oh yes they can become British..." Did I just notice a slight snigger in her voice?

"It's great. Isn't it?"

"Good for them," she said raising her voice slightly, perhaps in a bid to be more audible but I could sense that there was something unpretentious and slightly laden with emotion in her voice. She was turning slightly more red. "They can come from all over the place and become British. But I am English. I am English," she announced with a slight defiance. "Yes, they can come from all over the world. They can be British. I am English."

"That's right you know," I said. "There is a remarkable distinction there." I was getting a little more interested in the conversation but just then the grandson came and pulled her away to show her something. She excused herself. Her remarks kept ringing in my head. Technically she was right. The immigrants only became British citizens and not English natives. But how about the children of immigrants born right here on the soil of England, hadn't they become English too as well as being British? I wasn't sure Mrs. Bloomington thought so. Perhaps it was just the Brexit thing, where a wave of nationalism had swept the people to vote for the United Kingdom to be out of the European Union. Was it now receding into ethnic nationalism? I wondered how many felt like her. In my native land we called it tribalism. If only they knew it was a cankerworm. In my native land if a man was killed they would first check what his tribe was. Anyway, unlike the land of my birth the good thing here was that institutions were strong enough to deal with powerful individuals, as everyone was equal under the law, even those whose sole aim was to become ambassadors of violence. It was a pity how a land that was generous to other cultures could be turned into bomb-works by children whose parents had found their dignity in that land.

As I drove carefully, under the guidance of the google map, I got safely to the Town Centre at Wycombe.

It took me a while to get the automated ticket into the car park. I had to call a passerby to help. There were not that many vehicles. I meandered my way, parked the car and quickly found my way out of the parking complex into the mall. There were many shops in the mall. I was not interested in any window shopping. I did not really tell that many people that I was travelling abroad to avoid silly requests like "Please buy me a lap top" "What I want is an iPhone 11s" "Please get me an iPad and a Michael Kors wristwatch." Greatest Expectations! People in my native land still had this notion that the white man's country was a land full of gold and silver and once you crossed the shores, money could be found on the trees. Or that those items were as available as stacks of fruits in Benue State.

I wanted to watch a movie. Beauty and The Beast was showing featuring Emma Watson and Dan Stevens. I had watched the cartoon and wanted to watch this act. I love movies. I got myself a small size of popcorn and a bottle of water. I couldn't resist water any day as a drink. I had not factored in the irritating preludes in my rush. The adverts were just too many. I fiddled with my phone waiting for the movie to start.

"Movie was great. Wasn't it?" I said to a man I met at the restroom.

"Yeah. Yeah. A great musical. Fantastic how these stories never die and keep coming back."

"True. I think it's always so great to know that there is something beyond appearances," I said as we stepped out into the corridor, remembering how the courageous girl looked beyond the ferocious appearance of the beast to locate his kind heart.

"Even the tyrant has a kindness hidden somewhere in his heart. It's just to know where the switch is."

I bade him farewell and moved on.

3.

When I got to the car park there were so many cars now. For a moment I stood confused. What level did I even park the car? In my haste I didn't ram it into my head. Oh Gosh. Did I park at level 5 or 4?

I went to Level 5. The donated car had a remote for the doors. This one I drove did not. I searched around. I paced around a lot and began to get really uncomfortable. I was sure I was being observed through a camera. Thank God it was not the United States where being black was a terrible liability. I went down to Level 4 and 3 and came back to Level 5. I was sweating profusely. I thought of calling Yaks but then he said he would be holding a service at about that hour. Finally, I went over to a car I thought totally resembled it. I stood for a while looking at the number plate. I scratched my head trying to remember what it was. Even back home I didn't know my number plate, would it then be this car I just took for a drive?

As I inserted the key on the door a loud alarm set off. I panicked. I wanted to run away. But decided to stand there, looking foolish and quite confused. It was my own April 1st, my own Fool's day. No one needed to tell me. I was an outright fool.

The policeman drew out his gun as he came towards me. My hands were raised.

"I am not a thief please. I am just confused."

"Go down on your knees Sir, hands raised above your head," He said politely. I knelt down. My heart beat very fast. What if he wanted to do like the American cops who first shot to kill because the victim was black and could be dangerous? I had never been this afraid. He searched me and was satisfied I had no weapon.

"Let me see your ID."

My hands were trembling.

"I am a priest on holiday. Here's my international driver's license. I confused this car with my friend's which I drove here cos I don't know the number." I saw him relax.

He examined the license and my passport. "Which church did you say your friend is? Let's have the post code."

"St. Wulstans." I was roaming my line and had turned off data as it was quite expensive. I always had to use the Wi-Fi in the parish and in the public places. The police officer got the post code and the phone number and called severally. Yaks had a meeting that evening but should have been done by now. The call went into voice mail. I was calm now because I knew he believed me. In my native land, the police would have arrested me first and taken me to the station then a friend or relative would come and 'bail' me with a huge amount of money. At every police station it was posted on the notice board that bail was free but even if you were an angel that was mistakenly caught in the web of the police in Nigeria there was no way you were leaving without parting with some money. Bail was free in the sense that even if it was a murder that was committed the payment of a hefty sum could free you from prosecution and imprisonment.

Finally, the policeman offered to carry me to Hollis Road in High Wycombe. Yaks was standing outside chatting with a few members of the congregation. Of course, there was surprise and apprehension on everyone's faces.

"Nothing to worry about folks." The policeman assured. "Just a little confusion." He turned to Yaks. "What is the number plate of the vehicle your friend drove out?" Yaks told him. "And what color?" Yaks told him. He decided to come with us. As we drove down, I knew Yaks was embarrassed. I knew he would never give me his car keys again. What did I care anyway? It wasn't like back home where I had to have a car. Here I could live forever without one because I didn't really need one. Like I said, you could go anywhere with public transport.

 "Let's begin at Level 5," I suggested.

It wasn't long afterwards, we found the car.

As we drove back home quietly I knew that flawless as this society seemed to be I would still prefer the 'chaos' back home in Nigeria. I had gone from being a near terrorist at Heathrow to literally facing a one-man firing squad at a parking lot. If anything, these recent experiences were omens that I did not belong here. I would not fit in. I belonged to the heat, as a stoker of embers and letting them flame out to cook the lukewarm and careless attitude of officials into a hot sauce of action. And it was about time I took myself a little more seriously and relied more on that which had come to my rescue when all technologies and institutions had failed me. Grace.

BOOK SIX

JUST A LITTLE GODDESS

1.

I was summoned by mum.

She lived far away in Oban Town, a lush of green trees stretching as far as the eyes could see along a narrow road that meanders through the undulating terrain of hills and valleys made narrower each year by the creepy bushes that squeezed it into a narrow driveway. Oban Town was a place I did not miss when I stayed away and a place I did not want to leave whenever I arrived. I always had to battle to disentangle from the freshness of the air, the abstemious unhurried pace of things and the complete loss of consciousness of status. There, even when you had twelve degrees and a vault of dollars, a slay queen or magnate of sorts you were just a son or daughter of the soil. The old men dressed in the same shirts and wrappers as a week before sashaying along the streets and everyone making way and according respects without a care that they had no millions to their names. Maybe it was this egalitarianism that eschewed ambition from the people. They were simply content with being with that dose of sarcasm that laughed off everything.

Naturally I was filled with trepidation. I was mum's last child. Mum had no formal education so she would say I should not "mummy" her, that she is Mama; that if she was educated and sophisticated she would be 'Mummy'. She made a point of reminding me of her illiteracy each time I called her Mummy, as if she had chosen to rebel at being dressed in borrowed robes. Years ago, I was very broken about it and wept. I was sixteen. "Why can't I call you Mummy like all other kids call their mothers? Why? Why?" I demanded, letting the tears flow freely, holding my gawp in a fierce demand for answers. She knew I was not merely thinking aloud or being rhetorical, I really needed answers.

I saw the pain in her eyes and stopped crying when I noticed that her eyes welled up too. I moved closer and put my arms around her. "Mummy I love you," I said and closed my eyes.

"I say don't mummy me," she said, pushing me away unexpectedly and breaking down into a flood of tears. I began to cry again, gaining balance and holding onto her again trying to fathom the thing of once-upon-a-time that hurt my mum so badly that it made her shed tears whenever she recalled it. I held on to her as we cried together and I used my back palm to wipe her tears as a very palpable sensation of affection ran like spasms through my body. Oh gosh! How I loved my mum! Love was a visible thing indeed, solid like any material, heavy as lead though sometimes light and invisibly powerful like the infrared rays emitted by the sun. I still remember how I felt at that moment, light, large, heavenly like a doped girl. I let her cry her cry. She sobbed uncontrollably for a long moment and then stopped as if the tear glands had ceased their secretions. As a certain quiet enveloped us, I knew somehow that that would be the last cry, that is if I knew my mum well enough.

She had found her release.

"I really wanted to go to school. I was the first child but my father said it was better to save money and train my brothers. How much was it to train a child then?" She paused, letting the whole tragedy, the shortsightedness, the selfishness, the discrimination, the implications sink in. "And he trained all of them even my last brother who would repeat classes. I was sent to an Igbo woman in Aba to learn to trade."

I was speechless. Mum had never mentioned anything about this. I had always seen her as a goddess. Yes she was semi-literate. And so were many women of her age in the village. She had not sat inside the four walls of a school but her perspicacity was worth writing a Master's thesis on.

I followed mum to the room.

We sat on the bed together, nudging closer to her hesitantly at first and then leaning my head against her breasts. People said I took after Mum with a heavy chest. My friends teased me that when I walked my bosom and my buttocks squeezed me in between. Some said my buttocks came three miles behind me. Mum and I were that size of all dream girls, a well curved shape with commensurate height. I was beautiful and I knew it. With a pointed nose and sumptuous lips, I could dress up without a bra and yet the 'ladies' stand firm on my chest; I had a backside that many ladies paid heavily to enact through surgery. On top of that I could eat a cow and burn it all up in fast natural metabolism. But Mum had ingrained in me the idea that my body was sacred, otherwise the Virgin Mary would not be happy with me, just as she was sad about one of the kids she appeared to in Fatima who had worn a transparent dress that enticed men. Many men did business with Mum. It was only as I grew older that I knew that what they really wanted was her body. And Mum had a nice way of turning them into customers for her oil and spice business.

I had never seen Mum that vulnerable. I always thought it was because Dad dumped her that she worked as if she wanted to really prove a point. Mum had seen Dad through secondary school as young as she was. They had my first brother when Dad had not finished secondary school and had my other brother when Dad took a job with the postal agency after secondary school. Mum was pregnant with me when Dad went off to America for his degree. Mum still had the hope that Dad would return and formally wed her. All through the years Dad spent in America, Mum struggled and kept the family together, occasionally sending money to him.

Dad returned seven years later and told Mum they were not compatible. He had married a white lady they met at university although they had no kids. I remember how Mum wept every night for days. I would go and sit with her and weep as though I understood what it was all about. I was only eight. "He left. He left." She kept saying. And I would ask 'Who left Mama?" I didn't understand because all I knew was mum and my siblings. Other kids talked about their dads but I never knew what it was to have a dad and would tell them my dad was overseas. Then one night mum wiped her tears and said to me almost in a scary Arnold Schwarzenegger's voice, "No one has left. We're all here," and went to the bathroom to wash her face as if that was symbolic of a laundering of fears and pain. I noticed a vengeful strength in her thenceforth. I didn't know she had this other chronic pain about being refrained from going to school as a girl-child!

"But Mama you have done better than your brothers." I said, trying to console her. "They come to you to beg for money."

"Shut up. They don't beg. They ask. They are my brothers. What belongs to me belongs to them too." I was taken aback at this sudden defense of uncles I thought should be in the enemy camp, only to grow up to know that Ejagham people valued siblings above every other relationships, even their children.

"But they are men," I insisted stubbornly, in my teenage reasoning. "A man should not borrow from a woman."

"And who told you it's only the man that has to do well? If you like don't go and do well and think that your butt will save you," she said sarcastically but conciliatorily. "I keep warning you that a woman should not depend on a man for her livelihood but you won't hear. What would have happened to us if I had depended on your father?"

2.

That was twelve years ago, and now she was summoning me to the village for something I might only hazard a guess. Whatever it was, I knew she was missing me. Till twelve I could not sleep unless I slept on Mum's bed. I would put my hand in her bosom and then fall asleep. She had given up on me because as long as she was home, I wouldn't fall asleep until I put my hand in her bosom. Sometimes she would go to bed and pretend to be asleep so I would take the cue and go to bed and then I would wake up in the middle of the night and realize she wasn't there. I would go round the whole house looking for her and catch her taking stock and stay up until she was ready to go to bed.

Mum was a tigress at trade. She would go into the hinterlands, buy palm oil at low cost, stock and sell off at triple the price during off season. She would buy cocoa beans, palm kernel and all the local spices and send to her contacts in the North and make huge profits. Some of those villages had no access roads and you had to trek for miles in the forest. She would leave me with a cousin who lived with us, as my brothers were in boarding school; Mum sent all of them to a seminary hoping one of them would be a Catholic priest. When Mum returned I would be very sick because I could not sleep properly.

When I turned eleven Mum had a long talk with me and told me I had to grow up enough to take care of myself so she was sending me to boarding school. I could not even stay in the school for two weeks, they had to send me back to enroll in the community secondary school. Mum stopped me from using her bosom as an anesthesia if I had to continue sleeping on her bed. She made sure, without fail, that for nearly two hours before I went to bed, I would read aloud all I had learnt in school for the day. She thought that if you did not read aloud, you were not studying! I always looked forward to it because Mum sat there with gusto every night, listening, learning. I was forced to study to understand, and then to teach. And that is how I made an excellent result from a village school at my SSCE as well as making my mum know so much about what I learnt in school and how to read and write a little.

Mum was also a money lender.

Her astuteness was amazing. The revelation about her educational deprivation made me understand what drove her. She wanted to show that she could be better than the educated. It seemed to me that many successful people were just trying to fill a hole in their hearts. I fully understood why she treated my brothers a bit differently. She would scream at them whenever they asked for something but would give me all I did not need. She would tell them she did not want me to be tempted by boys. I grew up therefore with this sense, that no man could give me what I could not give myself.

Of course, I called her 'Mum' in my mind. It made me feel better. If she thought 'Mummy' was higher up and she did not deserve it, she was right, she deserved only something higher, to be a goddess, my little goddess.

I have tried to fence off this meeting but in that lovely autocratic manner Mum has insisted I appear by the weekend. She did not even think of the econometrics of it. I try now very much to limit my spending. Every month I transferred twenty percent of my earning into an 'escrow' account, as if it was a debt I owed someone. Indeed, it was a debt I owed my future. I took no money from guys no matter how broke I might be.

I dared not complain to Mum that I had no fare; she would ask who it was that kept all her money. I lived 700 kilometers away in Abuja and would need to take an airplane. I would also need to hire a cab to take me through the gruesome road to Oban Town, my village, unless a friend offered a lift when I landed.

I am Mum's only girl. I could hazard a guess why she was summoning me. She wanted to know why I was still single, why she has no grandchildren till date, whether there were no more men where I lived and worked bla bla bla.

The truth is, there is a scarcity of men. The city was full of boys, playboys. A real man is not afraid of commitment. These old boys were only ready to take a quick plunge and move on to the next girl. And the ladies had made it easier. If you delayed in opening your legs they branded you unserious and moved on or if they wanted to play along, would keep one or two side chicks pending when they would succeed in their quest; for someone had said that a typical man had two reasons to relate with a lady – to sleep with her and to know how long it would take to sleep with her. Many ladies panicked that the man would go away and did all his bidding in the hope of the man going down on one knee. Of course, when the man had enough, he would still walk away to another. So now ladies too beat men in their game and had several backup guys in case this one walked away.

How indeed was one to know that even if a guy appeared serious, he was truly serious? These guys had several coatings of honey on their tongues and seemed to compensate with sweet words the paltry account balances the economy bequeathed them. And how had we come this far to tie commitment to economics? Even when the economy was good, how was one to know that someone was the one? And I could count a number of friends whose marriages had gone sour only after a few months! Was it really possible to love one person till death? Rather than attempt and fail or become a punching bag as some of my friends had become was it just better to remain single?

3.

Maybe I was just afraid.

Mum always says I should not judge myself by her story, that there are good men and faithful men out there. Now at 29 how could I still wait with an open mind ? I had long promised myself not to live my life in waiting. I only need a man if he is available and I am quite fine if he is not.

I have a job with an online marketing company that drives me nuts. For the equivalent of five hundred pounds a month they take twenty-eight hours of my time a day. I have no life. Sometimes I get home too tired to even eat. Sometimes I sleep with my clothes on. I have this banging headache from hundreds of phone calls from clients and get woozy from staring at the iPad and the laptop. Well, the job comes with some perks, like travelling to China and Dubai. Maybe to an average girl that is exciting. Mum had made me go above average. I had spent two years doing a marketing Masters at Reading, UK and spent Mum's money touring European capitals during breaks. I had toured so much that trips did not really excite me anymore. During the two years I only holidayed back home once and not that I did not love to head home each break period; I realized that Mum did not expect me to! I had assumed studies in September and went home for Christmas only to notice that Mum was not as excited as I was to be home. I asked her what the matter was and nearly laughed when I got her explanation.

She believed that when you went abroad to study you

remained there until you finished. "Your father was overseas for nine whole years. He never came home although he visited the seventh year. He came home when he finished his studies. It's too far away to be travelling up and down," she told me. "And how would it seem when I boast to my friends that my daughter is schooling abroad and suddenly you appear?" I listened with a smirk on my face completely amazed at how there could be several perspectives to a matter one considered straightforward. What if I told her that some Nigerians worked in Nigeria and lived in London going home every weekend? What if I told her that some politicians went to France just to buy champagne or that some ladies boarded the plane to Paris just to buy perfumes? I concluded that, sometimes it was better to keep some myths alive.

"Okay Ma. You won't see me again until I finish school."

"Don't misunderstand me, it's not that I don't want to see you. I can't wait to have you all back to myself but you must concentrate and finish well." She told me of the first man to study abroad from Oban Town, how as a little girl she had to join the dance troupe to go welcome him. "He was gone for many years," she said.

I felt hurt a bit and rejected. Though I missed her, I respected her sentiments and used the time to visit Rome and the Vatican. I went to Toulouse and ended in Lourdes where the Virgin Mary appeared to a little girl called Bernadette. Then, I went to Lisbon and to Fatima. Fatima was that legendary place as kids we prayed to Our Lady of Fatima, Mum being a devotee of the Blue Army of Our Lady of Fatima. As a kid I imagined all those places, like Jerusalem, Canaan, Fatima to be in heaven above. Visiting those places were like returning from the dead; I never could understand when I heard that people went to Jerusalem. I thought those were consigned to the mysterious past when God walked with man physically. Of course, as I grew up I realized Jerusalem, Jericho, Fatima, they were places to buy and sell and drink and eat and steal and kill, as every other place on earth. But my childhood curiosity got the better of me and I decided to explore all those legendary places. The images of the nightly processions in Lourdes and Fatima still stayed with me. When I eventually returned and told Mum I had visited Fatima, she could have worshipped me. "Fatima! Oh Fatima !!" she kept saying and would revert the conversation back to Fatima as a little child asking the same questions in different ways. She brought me to share my experience in Fatima with her prayer group. I told her she could go to Fatima too, and she stood there entirely stupefied, wondering perhaps how on earth someone like her could visit such a hallowed place!

Till date Mum never compromised with her Wednesday Fasting, which is the day for Blue Army devotion. Back then when I was a kid there were two holy days at home, Sunday and Wednesday. On Wednesday she would meet in church with the group of women till noon, praying, fasting. Even now, if I didn't want to join Mum on her fast, I just had to make sure I wasn't in the village. She would wake up early and wash up all the pans and lock up the kitchen and announce "Today is Wednesday," as if anyone thought otherwise. Then she would begin to lock the doors, as if saying, 'The house is open after fasting.' It was this tediousness I resented about religion in my home. Mum shoved it at you in a take it or take it kind of way. When I protested that I was an adult she said a mother shows her children the ways of the world and the ways of the spirit and that she would not be found wanting in any as long as she remained my mother. Case closed.

It was providential that Mum ordered me to visit home because I myself was thinking of seeing her anyway. I have been contemplating leaving my job. In the recent past I have not stopped wondering what the purpose of work is. Why do we go to school only to become mere servants instead of creators? Look at Mum. And she never sat in a classroom, except for being my pupil.   Did I do an expensive Masters to come and kill myself over nothing? How would I do this kind of job and buy my own car and build my own house and yet I was even a 'high' earner! I know as a woman I am expected to mark time and wait for Mr. Right to come so that we would struggle together to acquire all those assets which would be attributed to him and when he gets tired of me sends me away and brings in another to enjoy the wealth we both created while I go and start afresh. I never really understood this loss of the middle class until I started working. How does someone work in her entire lifetime and all she can achieve is to pay the rent and feed herself and sometimes borrow to do so? Those who build own houses and own vehicles would only be business men or politicians or civil servants who have access to the public till because of the cash and carry economy that had no social safety nets.

 Maybe I could formally become Mum's manager and

end this drudgery although I would have to move the headquarters from the village.

4.

Mum didn't even know how much she was worth.

When I left secondary school I wanted to study medicine but the Joint Admissions and Matriculations Board gave me Business Management. After wasting a year in University of Calabar because of strikes, I switched over to a private university called Veritas where I graduated without hassles. There I met a classmate whose father dealt in palm oil. I went with her one weekend to meet with her dad and discuss some supply outlets. I knew that he agreed at first in the hope that he would have me as a side chick because I could see the way his eyes popped out in excitement when he saw me but eventually it remained a business relationship. That was how I closed the deal for Mum and she made entry into the West of Nigeria.

I am Mum's alternate. I sign all her accounts. I chuckled as I remembered how I made her to open a bank account.

I came home for the weekend during one of those strikes by the Academic Staff Union of Universities (ASUU) that made me leave the University of Calabar. I stumbled on Mum counting loads of cash in her room. I had the spare key and had opened the door because I wanted to drop my purse. She was somewhat embarrassed. I thought the large trunk boxes were filled with her prized clothing and jewelry. I did not know it was a decoy for a bank. I took time and found out all I needed to know, helping to count and arrange the money in neat stacks. The next day I left for Calabar and went straight to the main branch of First Bank. I waited to see the manager and told him I needed a bullion van to convey Mum's money from the village. I explained to him that Mum was an illustrious entrepreneur who was barely literate and didn't know much the value of banking. Oban Town was just an hour's drive from Calabar. I think I looked too serious and too desperate and perhaps too beautiful to be ignored so he offered to go with me. He got two gun-totting policemen as security. Meanwhile I had told Mum she should not go anywhere that some people from the school were coming to see her. Mum deferred to anything school. My brothers deceived her a lot about buying 'Apparatus' and 'Test Tube' and 'Amoeba' and she would give them money, which they would use and buy the latest fashion.

Mum nearly created a scene when she realized what I had done but she was calm when she saw the Policemen and probably feared for an arrest. The manager was a very nice man and spoke with great respect and assurance to Mum. The vehicle had a double cabin, so we were all conveyed to the city together. They took a passport photo of her and me to open the account. She had the equivalent of a little over 135,000 pounds in those trunks! Gee!

Five years later, while doing the compulsory national service, I opened a dollar denominated domiciliary account in Mum's name because I wanted to study in the US. I had this dream of buying a house in the US and bringing Mum to live with me. Without telling her, I would transfer money to a trusted Bureau de Change operator who would credit the account with the dollar equivalent. At 155 naira to a dollar, over time Mum had a balance of over one hundred and sixteen thousand dollars. When I could not go to Harvard, I applied to Reading. I had to open a pound denominated account in my name with a value of 45,000 pounds after explaining to Mum. I had not bothered doing any shopping because I knew I was going to get the best in London. I already had too many dresses although for a woman dresses are never enough. But when I got to the UK I realized that unlike back home, no one cared about how you looked so I ended up saving the money. Life was so shockingly simple and genuine in the UK that my vanity stuck out so glaringly. I loathed my consumerism. Back home some people were poor because they always lived beyond their means, in the UK no one looked up to another for his livelihood. But would I blame our people? In the UK the social systems took care of the poor whereas back home there was no social safety net. If you were poor back home, you were really poor, and that was why every rich person had hangers on.

The foreign accounts I opened paid back later, because when Muhammadu Buhari took over power, oil prices crashed further and the dollar became a very scarce commodity. I could not believe that one dollar was exchanging for nearly five hundred naira in the parallel market. As a management economics graduate, I knew that it could not be sustained. No nation would allow its currency become totally worthless. I knew this was artificial. We learnt that those with access to foreign currencies were colluding with parallel market operators to keep the naira worthless. People had become multi-millionaires overnight just by having access to forex.

What I wanted to do was, convert up to fifty thousand US Dollars and about ten thousand pounds into Naira at the prevailing rate at the parallel market, put the value in treasury bills for 180 days and watch things. But it took more than two weeks to get even five thousand dollars cash as the bank kept telling me to *"Come tomorrow."* The banks were out of cash as earnings from oil had dipped because of the Niger Delta militants' bombardment of oil pipelines. Also many investors withdrew their investments from Nigeria. There were all kinds of knee-jerk policies to shore up the naira. I had to reach out to my customer Alhaji Kolo who advised that I do a transfer to his account and he would credit my account with the naira equivalent although at a lower rate since it wasn't cash. At the end, forty-five thousand US Dollars fetched me a whopping sum of twenty-one million naira, while ten thousand pounds fetched me more than six million naira, all of which I promptly bought treasury bills with. I felt happy but quite sad. I had read in school that in the 80s the naira was equivalent to the dollar, and Mum had told me she used to send money to Dad, and it would be this our naira. I just couldn't believe how in the space of such a time a nation's currency had become so worthless. From the treasury bills, I was given 17% interest upfront, which I promptly put in an investment account in my own name. This was my own money, my ingenuity, not Mum's.

Sometimes I wonder where Mum had that wisdom of becoming a lender instead of encouraging dependency. Those who came to her for assistance she would say "I am not Moda Chrismas" and would ask what they could do with a little loan. And if you thought you would run away with her money she made you swear over a Holy Rosary and a Bible that you would return her money with interest. There was a legend about Mum of a man who borrowed money from her and died in an accident because it was past due date. There were some in the village who believed Mum had occult powers because they wondered how come she had never been swindled, as if it was the expected fate of every industrious person. Truth is Mum just so trusted in this her Virgin Mary thing that she believed she was invincible. She would always respond "Power pass power!" whenever she entered a gathering and was cheered 'Super Mama.'

When I returned from the UK I began to slack about going to church. After only three weeks I vehemently refused to join the Wednesday fast. I told her I was fed up with all the pretensions, because all those people who 'slept' in church had not stopped sinning.

5.

I think it was the unkindest thing I ever said to her till date. Mum was stung.

I knew because she became silent. I had hit her below the navel. I left to Calabar because I could not bear her silence. Itabang my elder brother had a one-bedroom apartment he shared with a live-in girlfriend. I had talked to Mum to get property in Calabar to no avail. I knew I would eventually have to force it on her once I saw a good deal. I was the educated part of her. Whenever Mum visited Calabar Itabang's girlfriend would vacate and Mum would sleep in the bedroom. Mum thought hotels were for prostitutes and would not hear anything about going to sleep in one. Adidi, Itabang's girl didn't have to move when I came around, although she made faces. One day I had to put a stop to it. "So sorry D-Girl," as I called her. "I couldn't attend the engagement."

"Which engagement?"

"Your engagement na. Hasn't my brother proposed to you yet ? I thought he did so two weeks ago?" I made as if I was cracking my brains.

"No o. He hasn't o," she said, loosening her guard. "Did he mention that to you?" she asked, sounding earnest and conspiratorial.

"Never mind." Just then Itabang walked in. "Tabs," I said, as I usually called him. "I thought you had done D-Girl's engagement? What are you waiting for? How can you allow a girl to live in with you when you haven't even done anything on her head? Don't you know you are cheapening her?"

"Sis leave that thing. We will cross that bridge when we get there."

"Na wao," I said with a shrug of the shoulders.

If she had any sense, as I was sure she had, I wanted her to know that she was cheapening herself by moving into a man's house when he had not even proposed, the kind of foolishness Mum had displayed then with Dad although it was different in their own time.   I saw that a lot in the UK, people living together and not marrying. But theirs was a post marriage society. Such life style had become a value for them. Even so they were less permissive. A girl stuck to her boyfriend no matter how distant they were. A girl would not think of having two boyfriends at the same time. But here it was such a normality to have multiple partners, even for married men. In the UK those who could sleep with anyone were found in night clubs or social media but here even a girl who considered herself decent could juggle between four different men! The most surprising aspect to me in the UK had been the fact that girls hardly dated above their age grades whereas here a girl of twenty had no qualms dating a forty-five-year-old man. Sometimes you would easily take a lady's husband for her dad. My two year stay in the UK made me realize that those in government in my country were actually spearheads, champions of an utterly bankrupt society. Only a bankrupt people allowed their kind to lord it over them.

It was during that prolonged stay with Tabs that I met my friend's boyfriend who owned the online business which eventually employed me and moved me to Abuja. I could not really understand how a man that was married would be a girl's boyfriend but that was their cud to chew not mine. Before I left to Abuja I had gone back to the village to tell Mum I was leaving for a job I got.

"Ekib sit down," she said, looking quite serious. She had not called me throughout our strike period and it had been nearly a month. And she was offering me a seat! I knew I was in for it, as I already anticipated anyway.

"Ekib why have you not stolen my money all these years?" She asked. I was totally taken aback. "Is it because you think I will call the police for you and arrest you?"

"No Mama. Why this question? Your money is mine na. Why would I steal it?"

"Now even if you stole my money would you stop being my child?"

"Mama I will not answer that. Do you think I want to run away with your money?"

I was angry.

"See Ekib." It was a serious matter whenever Mum addressed me by name. My name meant Gift, the full rendition being Ekib-Obasi, that is gift of God. After a line of male children, I was God's special gift to Mum. "I do my devotion not because I am good or bad but because God is my Father and the Virgin Mary is my mother. If I am good, I just try to be good not that I think it is because I am good that the Virgin Mary is my mother. Whether I am good or bad God is my Father. I just owe it to them to spend time with them. Whatever sacrifices I make, I do so because I feel I am loved not because I fear to be punished."

I knew then that I had really hurt her by those my remarks. However, the situation had helped push out a perspective I did not know she had. I wasn't a theologian but I felt that Mum had downloaded a whole theological package for me, a kind of guiltless religion where one was devoted to God as a child is devoted to parents out of a bond of love or blood, not fear, a bond which doesn't severe just because one has misbehaved. Maybe truly if people saw religion this way there would be more adherents especially in the western world.

"I am sorry Mam." I said and went to hug her. "I didn't mean to hurt you. I was just tired, you know."

Well, That was a little over two years ago. But it left a deep impression on me. I know Mum has done enough to make me form the habit of prayer, of fasting, of religion, as part of the ordinary context of things, the way it is natural for me to eat, to sing, to love. She has already succeeded but I did not want it shoved down my throat. I did not need anyone telling me about God or religion because it was already part of the supernatural me anyway. I knew I was more than me and those things were the access to the deeper me. They helped me reach the depths of myself and summon strengths and insights I needed. They helped me extend myself. I noticed a lot in the UK that people broke down easily over little emotional crises probably because their souls were paperweight. People saw the psychologist over a matter a spiritual connection could have resolved easily for them. I knew I was more than me because of the faith Mom had helped me build. In school friends wondered how I could be so fashionable and yet so full of faith, as if beauty was godless. The only problem was that charlatans in my country had turned faith into a multi-billion-dollar business and instead of 'to work is to pray' as someone said, it was now rather 'to pray is to work.' A few of those naira Pentecostal pastors had tried to bring prophecies to Mom's attention but she always responded that if anything was to happen to her the Virgin Mary would have told her beforehand. She would say "Mama Mary", as if the Virgin Mary was just standing next to her. Such a living dynamic faith was what I grew to see.

6.

We landed quite late.

We did not take off on time because the airline kept rescheduling the flight. There was aviation fuel crisis in the country. There was always some form of fuel crisis or the other even when Nigeria was a major producer of petroleum. After the first set of refineries were built no successive government did anything about building other refineries. Each year millions of dollars were spent on what was called turn around maintenance (TAM). Before they went into power politicians would promise to take drastic measures that would put discipline in the oil sector but as soon as they got into office they realized they needed to be reelected and elections needed money and money came from all those bogus oil contracts. They also realized they had to become dollar millionaires and it came from all those sources. So, refineries were mostly always down and fuel needed to be imported and figures conjured on local consumption rate which enabled the national oil company to allocate money which was easily pulled out through claims of fuel import. At a point it got so bad that ships would claim to land with petroleum products, get profiled and then would go without off loading, only to return a few days later to make claims of a new delivery. Some docked empty ships and claimed the cost of a fully loaded tanker. Thus, sometimes there was a real scarcity even of aviation fuel. Gradually because of the mismanagement many foreign airlines had turned to Ghana as a hub for their fuel as Nigeria was not reliable. You had to have strong connections to be an oil thief. And so foreign exchange was wasted on these ventures of importation that very little percentage of the budget was left for infrastructure. The deals were so lucrative that no persons in government really wanted the situation to change. The hope was that when the private refinery in Lagos became fully operational, things would change for the better.

I still had to hit the road to Oban that evening. It was already late but hopefully I should be in Oban by 8pm. I would have to get to the Goodluck Jonathan by-pass built by Liyel Imoke and hire a cab that would take me to Oban. If only Tabs had a car it would make things much easier. I used up all the rhetorical skills I had to make Mom buy a car but she would not. She would not dare drive, she said. I told her she could get a driver but she said it was for big people. Somehow mom was still influenced by all her childish awes. For her a car was symbolic of a certain status which she did not see herself as attaining yet. She felt that those who had cars had money to overflowing. Well somehow it helped her pass away as an ordinary woman when indeed she was worth more than many of those men and women who drove flashy cars. Even my brothers did not know how much Mom was worth otherwise they would have designed schemes to milk her dry. Somehow this her not going to school made her feel as if she was really less than the goddess she was.

I became apprehensive when I saw Mom. Though we hugged and embraced for a while and she made her traditional complaint about me getting thin, I noticed a certain awkwardness bordering on a level of anxiety. I could not place my hand on what it was. If she had something to scold me about her demeanour would be different. She would be in a place of power. But she looked vulnerable, almost as if she needed my buy in. Maybe she had made a wrong investment and it backfired and she was apprehensive telling me about it since I had advised her to consult me first before such decisions? I could not wait to hear what it was. Okot a cousin that lived with mom was nowhere to be found. I dragged my bag and mom towards the room.

"I can't wait to hear what it is o," I said.

"Have you eaten ? Eat first. I made your favourite for

you."

"I hope someone is not trying to bribe me o," I said with a titter.

"Go away," She said a bit awkwardly. "Who will use her money to bribe herself ?"

"As in Powerful Mama."

"Power pass power o my daughter!"

She had set the food at the dining. She would not use the dining to eat. It was too formal for her. She preferred to sit on a low stool in the kitchen and eat her food. Whenever I was around we ate together but when I ate alone I preferred the dining. I had paid for the dining table and brought it home one day. There was a table there originally but it was heaped with goods along with the entire dining section of the house. I had to persuade mum to condemn one of the rooms to a store and move the table into that room with additional shelves for other goods. It was a five-bedroom bungalow, with each of us having a room to ourselves. My room was just to pile my dresses and shoes as I practically slept with mum in her room. My brothers hardly visited the village anymore and mum was left with Okot my cousin to do with the two rooms as he pleased.

Mom was grinning from ear to ear as she watched me eat.

The meal was really delicious. It was *Orang'e mbid*, a traditional menu of pounded coco-yam foofoo with a spicy slightly oily sauce without vegetables called *Isu-nchage*. You could eat the foofoo with other sauces such as Isu-m*funi*, *Isu-nkon*, *Isu-aje* but nothing compared to a ball of *orang'e mbid* dipped into *isu-nchage* and let to glide majestically down the pharynx. The only danger was that when you were done eating, because you were always tempted to eat more than your capacity, you entered the default mode of the python when it swallowed a prey. Mum had taken care too to add melon balls in the sauce which she often had baked and stored in the local oven. It was a delicacy of mine from childhood. When I was in the UK I didn't waste my time trying to familiarize with British food. I did not know if they even had typical foods at all. Thank God African stores were all over the place and I always ensured I cooked myself a good meal. My residence became a sort of rendezvous. My classmates found it quite amazing how I had a balance between my academics, being homely, of faith and being altogether fashionable.

Mum knows I sleep like a log of wood. I was tired from the journey, what with the long wait at the airport, the rough ride on the pot-holed road and then the heavy meal! Whenever I felt sleepy I was quite fluent in gibberish. Those who know me well enough are careful to leave me alone to nap for a while so I clear my head. I dozed off on the chair because I wanted the food to digest properly before I would go and lie down. Mum knows I am prone to acid refluxes if I eat and go to bed immediately so she would allow me nap sitting up for a while before she would tap me to go to the room. It must have been around 11pm that I stood up from the chair to go into the room.

7.

Mum was startled when she saw me. I had not worn shoes and had hardly made a noise as I swung the door open. She was sitting on the bed, supporting her right cheek with her hand in an obviously pensive manner. Sleep took flight immediately from my eyes as I saw her that way even as she pretended to snap out of it.

"*Mam* what is it? *jen efabe*?" I said, going quickly to sit on the floor under her feet and staring up at her. "Are you worried about me? I will marry you hear. Don't worry," I said stroking her legs.

"It's not about you. It's about me. I am going to wed," she said suddenly.

"What!"

I sat there momentarily confused, transfixed, moping, as the information sank in.

"Wed?"

"Yes," she said hesitantly. "I wanted to let you know first."

How old was mum even? Fifty eight? Sixty? Marriage? To serve what purpose? For as long as I had known mom I was not sure she had used her vagina for anything else than to pee. She told me that during her time circumcision was for both male and female but that when I was born word had already gone round that the clitoris was not meant to be mutilated because it enabled women enjoy sexual intercourse. While many women insisted on going ahead to mutilate their daughter's she had left mine intact and only hoped that it would not make me become a girl of easy virtue of sorts. Luckily I have grown up knowing that sex is very much a thing of the mind and something I could will away if I didn't want.

"Are you sure about this ? You have lived your life independently and have done quite well. Do you now need a man to come and take control of you?"

I genuinely wanted to know if it was something she

really wanted to do or if one of those honey tongued, naira digging men with infrared eyes had perceived her financial status and wanted to harvest where he did not sow. I stood up and paced about the room, leaning on the wall and pulling slowly at my hair with my right hand. In the distance the petrol generator was humming. It was usually somewhat slightly hypnotic and could lead me to nap in the afternoon. Mum scarcely used the gen except she had guests or when any of us was around because we would insist she buy petrol for use every day. Government had finally brought electricity to the village from the grid but the electric poles fell so very often that days and weeks sometimes went by without power. Later it was discovered that a village of settlers where the control was stationed had the habit of its young men going to switch it off just to show they could hold Oban Town inhabitants hostage as the grid passed over their village without stepping down electricity for them. Whenever we filled the petrol tank, the gen could last till 5am and go off on its own if no one heard its final squeaking.

"Mam. I'm so confused. I don't even know why you would want to marry at this time."

"So I am too old to marry ?"

"No na. That is not what I am saying. It's just too much for me right now. I can't really understand."

"Well, I also want to wed. I want to wear the wedding dress and stand at the altar."

"Seriously ma ?"

"Yes na. It has always been my dream to wear the wedding gown and be properly wedded. All those women who got wedded do they have two heads? " I burst into tears as I saw mum tear up. And I rushed up to her and held her and began to cry uncontrollably for all her botched dreams and all the ones bottled up. We grow with a vision of ourselves and a hope that we would be what we wish to be but life turns and pushes us in different paths like a strong wind that sways the aircraft from its route and yet like a plane landing safely despite a rough flight we hope somehow to arrive at a safe place. I could not stop mum from dreaming and wishing her dreams came true. No one is too old to dream, to be self-fulfilled. She was not even old. If she wanted to be a bride who was I to stop her?

"Mam I love you," I was saying. "Anything you want that will make you happy, I'm by your side. But know that I love you just as you have been. A woman does not wed herself. You were there always ready but none of them was man enough to stand up to you. Not even dad could stand a hardworking beautiful woman like yourself and so he developed a complex and ran off to marry a white woman. Be a bride if you must but you've been more than a bride, you have been both a bride and groom in all these years. You have been a goddess. I love you mama."

It was moments like this that the magnetism between me and mum became so intense that I felt like finding a way to be gulped and routed back to her womb. In all this I had not asked mum who the man was; whoever he was I would do my best to ensure mum was protected. We would not work hard all these years and hand things over to a man to play pontiff.

"Won't you ask who the man is?"

"I know you will say it eventually but for me it is immaterial. Since it appears that it is more of what you want than what the man wants, I am in to it no matter who is involved."

"Well. It's your father."

"No way!" I sprang up. "When? How? What of his white woman? is he going to marry two wives?" I needed answers and needed them quickly as my heart beat accelerated.

"Your father has come to see my brothers twice and has apologized to them. My brothers have asked me to accept him back but I told them under one condition, that he wed me in the church! He has agreed. He has also agreed to do the complete traditional wedding before the church wedding."

"What of his white woman?"

"My brothers said he told them that the woman says she is going away. You know men. I hear that she saw nude pictures of a lady in his phone and the messages he sent to her so she decided to go away and is asking your father to pay her a huge sum of money."

"So, he is coming back because he will soon be broke? Nonsense man."

"Shut up. Stop that. He is your father. That is not respectful."

"Leave me o. Leave me alone. Is it now that he is broke that he remembers us?" I stormed in anger and left the room.

In fairness to my father he had tried for us to have a relationship but I was never forthcoming. I learnt that there were people who could feel the kind of pain Jesus felt on the Cross and they would bleed, they were called Stigmatists. As I grew up to understand what my father did to mum I bore her pain in an immediate way and it injected me with such umbrage that the very thought of him made me want to smash his head. While I was studying at Reading he had invited me to the US and I only accepted because I wanted to visit Disneyland because he was one of their engineers. I did fly to Orlando Florida with my own ticket. I spent five of the seven days I stayed with them going to several of the theme parks in Disney. I did not hide the fact I agreed to go at all because of Disneyland. I wanted him to know that he was not the only one that could use and dump people. At the end we did not even have a good conversation. All I talked about was Disneyland. We all went out to dinner once and I was merely being polite. Ellen his wife tried to be nice and I was nice to her too but I made sure she realized there was a wall between us that she could not penetrate. I left them after a week and went to New York where I spent a week going round the shops, visited Ground Zero and the United Nations and spent nights at Times Square. Whenever he called I would answer impersonally and he would round off the call because of its awkwardness.

I was so used to being without a dad and so okay being only with a mum that it would have to be a new experience entirely. I was used to being taken into confidence by mum and being her chief adviser and manager and now what? Dad had left his job in the US because he was given an appointment to head an agency of the federal ministry of technology. After only two years I read in the papers that he was sacked because of corruption! That was during the presidency of Goodluck Jonathan. I believed what he told Toks my brother though that he refused to play along in a deal and he was set up. He wanted to use American standards to run the place not knowing that in Nigeria the standard business ethic is corruption. I was not interested in knowing how he wriggled out of the matter but I knew that the new government gave him several contracts which he handled and had made his way into the company of many prominent politicians and government officials. Ellen had gone back to the US in the middle of the scandal and he had to travel down regularly. I wouldn't know at what point she caught him cheating with his phone.

As I sat on the couch that whole marriage thing spurned around in my mind. Perhaps because my father had married a white woman he would be more inclined to seeing marriage as a partnership? But would he even respect mum who by his standards was not educated, he who had even acquired a doctoral degree? Some African men see marriage as sole proprietorship, as a monopoly where the commodity is the woman. The man could of course have other 'investments' but the woman had no say, always to be available, offering herself and her resources to eternal credit to the man who sometimes had nothing else to contribute than the fact that he paid the bride price and therefore bought and owned the woman. It is said the good Lord made them male and female; they were made to go hand in hand, for one to feel the other's pains and joys but some African men now made it seem as if being married was a cultured way of buying a slave.

I was consoled at the fact that among my people the woman had due liberties; only the Ejagham woman herself would choose to remain where she was oppressed because whenever a woman was being married out, especially to non-Ejagham grooms, her siblings would tell her to return home if she was no more valued or if she felt oppressed. Only that sadly I noticed that the men allowed the women to become bread winners while they went about drinking themselves to stupor. Hopefully dad had become differently socialized because of his exposure.

8.

I did not even know when I slept off. I woke up to the hubbub of mum's preparation to go for the early morning mass. I checked the time. It was 5.15am. Mum would usually shower before going to mass which usually started by 6am. It took approximately ten minutes to walk to church. She would pray first as soon as she woke up then do her toilet before heading down to church. In the UK I had joined the habit of having a bath only in the evenings; in the morning, we would wake up, brush and wash our faces, armpits, back and front, spray body mist and perfume and dress up for classes. Sometimes I forgot to bath in the evening when I returned from lectures, especially during the cold periods. I could not really do that here in Nigeria because of the humidity. There was just something about a bath in the morning that completely refreshed and removed that staleness of spirit.

I went to my own room to have a quick shower. I had sold the idea to mum to set the house as a hotel, where there would always be toiletries in every bathroom and towels – for feet, hands, face. One of the duties of a cousin who lived with mum was to ensure absolute hygiene. Mum was a very neat woman despite having lived in Aba in her early years so she always kept the house clean in spite of Okot's tardiness. I would have to return from church to do my makeup. By 5.47 I was ready and was just in time to see mum step out of her room. We walked to

194

church as she led in the rosary. I could feel she was very pleased that I was accompanying her.

The Priest was ten minutes late for the Mass. I could vaguely recognize him. He had grown a white beard and now wore rimless spectacles with a completely bald head. The late start of the Mass gave the small congregation a chance to finish off with the rosary which they would normally recite before mass and stop as soon as the priest made his entrance. He seemed a bit distracted at mass for no reason.

I know I have this effect on Priests when they meet me for the first time because I am quite a regular in church even on weekdays and the bold ones always want to find a way to make acquaintances. I am beautiful and conscious of it but I do my best to not lead them into temptation even though I could see from their eyes that they would willingly fall. They get quite excited when I agree to stop by for a drink but I carefully put a ring around me that fences off all passionate desires. I know they want friendships and the company of the opposite sex sometimes and I do that without compromising myself so at the end when we become real friends, some of them would open up and call me "419". In Nigeria 419 means advance fee fraud and is the generic term for all kinds of deceptive behavior; in my own case they tell me to my face that when someone sees me it would seem I were already mincemeat not knowing that I am an impossible palm kernel to crack. This was more amusing in Abuja where as soon as men knew I am a 'Calabar girl', they would thank their stars and assume that I was already theirs. Calabar girls have a reputation to be sexy, homely and perhaps an easy catch but they always got disappointed with me and sometimes angrily told me

I was a fake Calabar girl. As for the priests it was never that serious. Many of them became friends with me because I appreciated their humanity without taking them for granted. One would tell the other how friendly I was and that one would come to try to become friends too, and often I was invited to sit out with them. I would go and we would drink together and I would tease them about anything and they always seemed pleased because they could lose their guard and not be uncomfortable. I never judged them. Sometimes I would call up the most ludicrous one among them and book an appointment for confession. They were always happy that in spite of my friendship with them I still had enormous regard for their priestly ministry. They would openly tell me about their friends who were girls and sometimes allowed me to meet them. Like I said I never judged them but there was a way I related with them which impacted on them and some of them would discuss very personal challenges with me and seek my opinion. I knew over fifteen of them and none had not a girl that was not close to them. What I was not sure was whether they were having sexual intercourse because on one of those occasions, as it was only on Sundays that I had the time, five of us had hung out so late that they suggested we all sleep in their colleagues' residence. Everyone was tipsy. I actually slept in the priest's room and on his bed. He wanted to lay a duvet on the floor and sleep there but he had a large bed that could take four so I asked him to not mind sharing the bed after all we were all adults and civilized by our faith. And we slept peacefully. I attended mass the following morning before I left. So, I would not know if the girls that accompanied priests to their residences had limits or not because I had mine and the priest had made no attempt whatsoever to harass me.

9.

The morning mass was over.

I wanted to stay back and pray a bit but mum came to me, tapped my shoulder and beckoned on me to follow her. I knew she wanted me to meet the priest.

Everyone was delighted to see me and I was nearly squeezed out like a sucked orange fruit with all the hugs and pleasantries from the local women. "Chei. This one is really a carbon copy of her mother o," one of the women said, as if she was knowing me for the first time. Well, I had not been to the village church for the near two years I left to Abuja so it was understandable.

Mum waited patiently for the women to be done admiring and checking me out and then requested me to accompany her to the priest's residence. The residence was about a hundred and fifty meters from the church.

The priest was eagerly waiting for us. Apparently, mum had told him she was bringing me. He seemed to have a good reputation in the community and a good mixer with the local people. He seemed to be in his early fifties and by his short homily that morning, seemed quite focused.

"Morning Father. I hope you are enjoying our village," I said, extending my hand in greeting.

"My sister, what will I do? It's my community too by the way."

"Ah so you are not enjoying the place."

"Nooo. I mean that the only choice I have is to enjoy

it," he said laughing. "Please o, before Powerful Mama will sanction me." Mum seemed pleased by the flattery.

"So Fada this is my daughter the one I told you is in Abuja. Ekib meet Fr. Itanja."

"Pleased to meet you Father," I said, shaking hands again and bending one knee slightly in respect.

"Call me Fr. Ja. You are on leave?"

"No Father. I took some days off. This woman summoned me."

"Ah. Na Powerful Mama o. You must to obey," he said laughing. Mum was grinning. As we chatted along mum seemed a bit cut off from the conversation.

"Ekib let me go and prepare breakfast. Take your time."

"Mam. Don't bother with me. I think I will have breakfast with Father Ja," I said.

"Okay o."

I could see that he seemed a bit surprised at my hutzpah. That was how I would break into their guard and fish their real selves out.

"So, what would you like? I want to have *dodo* and fried eggs." *Dodo* was a favorite Nigerian menu of fried ripe plantain slices.

"That is my best breakfast." I said.

"Would you like tea or coffee?"

"Fr Ja you be real oyibo o. Anyway, I will have coffee."

"Great. Me na village priest now o." It was funny the way he said it. "But how come I never met you when I was in Abuja? Anyway I hardly visited home so I wouldn't know our towns people who were in Abuja."

"So you are back finally home ?"

"Yes. I finished my tenure at the NGO and Bishop assigned me here a few months ago."

"I heard about your kidnap."

"Yes o. That was a horrible experience but God used it to strengthen my faith. I believe totally in God."

"You didn't ?"

"My dear, faith is dynamic. Sometimes it is so turgid, at other times it is so laxed but if you are lucky God brings events into your life that serve as a booster each time you feel a lax."

"True." I drank my coffee as the sweet aroma of the fried red plantain slices and egg filled everywhere and whetted my appetite.

"Your mum told me about the reunion. Isn't it great? God is wonderful. He works in mysterious ways," Fr Ja was saying. "Can you imagine that after over two decades your parents are coming back in grand style! The only sad thing is that your mum says your dad wants the wedding in the city. The traditional will be in the village of course but the wedding will be in the city. I would have loved it to be here so they could see our church and perhaps assist us. Here we have very little to celebrate. That would be a great joy to the community."

I did not know they had gone this far. I lost my appetite immediately. I was not sure whether the priest was subtly asking me to play an advocacy role and bring the wedding to the parish or he was just helplessly complaining. My father had links with the politicians in the state and it would really be a rendezvous for politicians who controlled the resources of the state and sometimes played a patronizing role by making donations when they were invited to churches. I guessed he was just complaining because he had no way to know I could do anything about it.

I was angry. I excused the priest, brought out my cell phone and called my dad. I put the phone on speaker and placed it on the table as I wasn't with my ear piece. I hear taking the phone too close to the ear had some negative radiation effects.

"Good morning Daddy."

"Good morning honey."

"Daddy don't honey me please. So, you and mum you have been planning your thing behind us. On top of that you want to take the wedding to Calabar. That is not going to happen."

"What is not going to happen? The wedding ? "

"If a wedding will take place at all, it is in Oban."

"But Oban…"

"What is wrong with Oban daddy?" I screamed. "You either take it or leave it." I switched off the phone knowing he would try and call back. For a moment there was an awkward silence. I lost every sense for food. How come that in one instant one was hungry and in another so slaked without a morsel passing through the lips! Those who thought humankind were mere flesh and blood were truly mistaken. There seemed to be a constant interplay between the body and spirit such that sometimes when the body was hungry the soul fed it without any physical food and when the soul was hungry the body fed it with material.

"Oh my. I am so sorry," Fr. Ja said bewildered. "I hope I didn't cause any trouble?"

"Father don't worry. But just tell me please. Did my mum ask you to talk to me?"

"Well, Yes. I actually asked her to invite you down. I figured the best way was to put it in that beneficial tone so that you would feel a sense of obligation to the community. But you have even gone farther than I thought. Is your dad not going to be offended ?"

"Offended ? Did I feel offended when he abandoned us all those years ? Let him just try me and see. He would not dare. Do not worry Father. Just start preparing for the wedding. He should bring all those his big politician friends to get sick on this road as well."

Fr. Ja laughed awkwardly and said poetically "This is the road traversed less by many except shepherds of souls." And then added that "But I hear the Archbishop is the one to celebrate the wedding."

"The Archbishop should come to Oban. Father do you want the wedding or not?"

"I want o," and we both burst out laughing at the way he said it.

"But will your dad really change the venue and bring it here?" he asked after a while, doubtfully. "Hasn't he gone too far in the arrangements? I don't want to be the cause of any family feud. Maybe you let it ride."

"Don't worry about it father. It has nothing to do with you. What kind of arrangement is that in which I do not know anything about and I am the only daughter! As much as I am certain the sun will rise tomorrow, my father will bring the wedding to Oban because at this point this is what I want. He must. For peace to reign. He must even be relieved that he has my blessing."

"Blessing?" Fr. Ja asked, with a slight squint. I knew what that almost imperceptible scoff meant. He was wondering who it was that should give the blessing to the other. Nothing could compensate for the fact that he left to America when I was still being formed in the womb only to return and declare us unworthy of him. Now he would have to deserve being worthy of us and I had just set this as one of several conditions. I stood up to leave.

"You have not eaten your food at all."

"I am so sorry Father, I lost my entire appetite. Please forgive me. Usually I am a very good eater but I have suddenly become full," I said with a grin. "I am sure it will not be wasted."

"Not to worry. This is why my mum used to say we should allow someone to finish his meal before breaking whatever news."

"It's alright really, Fr. Just that all those memories came back, the years my mum struggled all by herself to keep us together, to train us, to be both father and mother to us all."

"Here." Father Ja handed a tissue to me to wipe my eyes. "I believe everything happens for a reason. It's never late to make things right. Even if you think your dad abandoned you, nature, the spirits, the universe did not. See what your mum has made of herself and you all. Isn't it great that the great puzzle is now coming together to make sense? I think we should give more credit to your dad than we are now because he still had the choice of going with someone else. It means his mind was always with your mum. Just look at this on the bright side."

"Thank you father, have a pleasant day."

As I went away the words kept recycling in my mind as a refrain. *It's never late to make things right... It's never late to make things right... It's never late to make things right...*

I did not really know what he was coming to make right. There had been nothing wrong with my mum and I. We were just fine. Mum had always been disposed and if there was any grace accompanying, she already had it. He it was that needed to make things right for himself and to open the channel of grace for himself. But as it would help mum live out her fantasies, that was great, I would be happy because of her. Perhaps there was something fun about being a chief bridesmaid after all, the position would not be contestable. I was the sole candidate. I had always declined being made chief bridesmaid but now the onus fell squarely on me and I would do it for mum.

BOOK SEVEN

EMIR OF ONITSHA

1.

My head was banging. I didn't feel like seeing anyone but having a colleague turn up from town in the evening like this, I had no choice than to play host.

"I think it is malaria, the way I am feeling."

"Feeling that you don't need to do a test first ?"

"First things can come last sometimes you know..."

"But you know that it could be something else."

"Something else like what?"

"Something like malaria Fr. Itanja! But you can't escape from doing a test to confirm," he persisted as he switched on the ignition. It was already 8pm but he insisted on making the one hour drive to the city along the lonely road. My head was swirling as if I was drunk. I really felt sleepy and tired and had dozed off briefly in the middle of sentences until Fr. Ojong realized the conversation was going nowhere. I could still pick the substance of what he wanted. He had come to solicit my support for a youth project he was embarking upon. I had been assigned to my native locality as I returned from my years of service at the nation's capital and he wanted to explore my skills and contacts in the development sector.

"Okay. I will have a test done first thing tomorrow.

Have a safe trip." I sleep-walked to my bed.

****

2.

I was at a grand reception. I had just turned 70. I was pulling softly at my white brimming beard. It was the classic feature I had come to be known with since my 50th birthday anniversary, which with a completely permanently shaven head and rimless spectacles, gave me a stoical countenance, except that I was not as smallish as Ghandi, with my 95 kg weight. A committee of friends from all my previous parishes had come together to put up the party. I insisted that the celebrations go back to where I was ordained, in Oban Town. Oban held my heart hostage. Each time I visited, an affinity was created with the shrubs of greenery and the distant quiet regard of the stretch of hills that mounted an eternal guard of honor.

70! How did it really feel like? Strangely I did not feel old. I only realized I was not as strong as I was twenty years earlier. I often had to remind myself that I was turning 70, because in all practical senses I still felt like a young man. I wondered really whether this was the reason many elderly men behaved like kids!

The committee had bought me a driverless vehicle and also given me a ticket to spend two weeks in London. Driverless vehicles were the toy of the rich in Nigeria. The automated-steering technology used for parking had been extended with cruise control to build the framework for the driverless. Mine was a Google driverless, with a rotating roof-top Lidar, a camera that used "an array of 32 lasers to measure the distance to objects to build up a 3D map at a range of

200m" so that the car could identify any hazards. Another camera, one that sees through the windscreen had ability to read road signs, detect pedestrians and other vehicles; meanwhile radar mounted on the front and back bumpers monitored vehicles in front and behind. An aerial mounted behind collected geo-location info from satellites while an ultrasonic sensor on the right rear wheel measured the car's movements. Inside the car were altimeters, gyroscopes and a tachometer that helped to measure the rev of the engine. All these gadgets inside and outside combined to make the driverless car an efficient and safe vehicle. I had driven in a few during my trips overseas, just for the fun of it but I never knew I would be receiving one as a gift from friends. Why do friends of spiritual leaders often give them expensive material gifts?

But trust me, having self-driven a car for more than forty-five years, I could not just entrust myself to a computer to take me around. So, I made arrangements for a buyer so I would donate the proceeds to the diocesan motherless babies' home. What with the chaos that was characteristic of the driving in most Nigerian cities! No matter how smart a computer was, it would not know how to navigate the rush hour chaos when traffic lights were down and traffic police were nowhere to be found; how does the driverless know that it could beat the one way and even drive in the opposite direction of the road, and on the wrong lane, if you had to get home at all? How would it know how to respond when angry motor cycle riders came quite close and slapped the car in anger as if it would feel any pains, as a way of venting their rage against the system?

Crude oil prices had been on a regular downward spiral since many countries banned the production of fossil fuel vehicles. Naturally Nigeria had opened her arms to receiving used fossil fuel vehicles that came from Europe and the USA, becoming a ready dumping ground in an extension of a second-hand economy. Tiny nations like Rwanda had it right from the onset when they banned the importation of used vehicles and gave incentives to those who imported brand new vehicles but Nigeria on the other hand crafted an automotive policy that placed 100% duty on new vehicles and 75% on used vehicles. Rather than encourage assembly plants, the policy impoverished Nigerians all the more, because as long as you wanted to buy a vehicle, it was most likely going to be a used one which had been quite beaten down by the original user and bought quite cheaply by the importer who would then pay 70% duty on it. Elsewhere the future of the earth looked bright as breakthroughs in technology were minimizing use of fossil fuels. But Nigeria was in a world of its own, with millions priding themselves with fuel guzzling limousines. More than a decade earlier Dangoddey refinery in Eko had completely taken care of domestic consumption and eliminated the vicious corruption cycle of petroleum imports. The way the country had been run, it would probably have been better to privatize governance and give it to Dangoddey to run for everybody's profit, except that he had a due bias for his religion and used his profits mostly to cater for the poor of his region and religion. I often wondered why it was that those who belonged to some faiths had such restricted sense of humanity, and even if they became trillionaires, were mainly concerned with the poor of their faiths!

Anyway I used my 70th birthday ticket gift for the two week trip to London. But the two weeks ended up being five years and counting. I didn't choose to be an illegal alien, I could not just go back home because of the Armageddon that had struck with the takeover of government by terrorists.

3.

The year was 2033.

I still could not believe it that Onitsha, the great city of commerce and Catholicism by the River Niger had now capitulated and become the sub headquarters of the caliphate. Like a dream the Holy Ghost Catholic Cathedral had its towers adorned with minarets, its altar demolished, and the holy paintings and sculptors destroyed completely. The church had been a mosque for more than four years running. There was now an emir at Onitsha, himself a fierce brutal warlord who had made a demonstration of his powers by publicly executing those who refused to convert to the new religion. Out of fear for their lives, many people had recanted Christianity and become adherents of the terrorist religion. Many rationalized that life was more important and it was the same God so there was no need to lose one's life when one could help it. Some others claimed they were still Christian at heart and that what the Lord Jesus demanded most was the heart and he should better know that they loved him right in their hearts even if they now had to pray many times a day and squat to pee.

The news had come to me as a shock. I felt guilty staying back in London while my people suffered and died in their droves. I felt like a coward, like a runaway captain from his ship. And yet if we believed in the providence of God, there was a reason for all this and a reason I had escaped it all, a reason it all blew out as soon as I left the shores of the most populous black nation. I so desired to be back and face it all after all at 75, I had done my time, what more was I alive for?

When it blew out the international community made an outcry and threatened to expel the country out of the United Nations. Economic sanctions were slammed. African Union stopped sending peacekeeping troops after the first batch was roundly executed by the fundamentalist State commanders of *Eihad Aljana* or Servants of Paradise (SOP) who were now perfectly aligned with Islamic State of West Africa and Boko Haram. Some drones killed a few SOP and Boko Haram commanders and some civilians as well, and that was much that could be done. Now most of the pressure was from diaspora Muslims and Christians like myself who kept crying to the international community to do something.

The voice of the international community was not as strident as it used to be. After the Brexit and the rise of nationalism, the United Nations became more a talk-shop. The British Parliament had made laws to legitimize Sharia and allowed for a Sultanate alongside the Crown due to pressure from British Asians who were now the majority in the land. The British Prime Minister was Muslim, just as majority of members of parliament including the House of Lords.

In the United States, after eight years of Donald Trump and a double tenure of the grandson of Bush Jnr, the president of the United States was now an American born Arab whose parents were Syrian refugees. In France both the President and the Prime Minister were children of Arab migrants who had done a good job of nurturing the seeds of the faith in their children. While other populations allowed the budget to determine the number of children, the Arab migrant Europeans continued to marry and beget the maximum of children. As at this time Asian migrants and therefore people of the Holy Faith outnumbered others by a ratio of 3:1. Unlike other populations that had either lost their faiths or allowed it to become merely nominal, families of the Holy Faith gave compulsory religious instruction to their children for years as an after-school initiative, during which time they could recite the entire Holy Book. While many Christians hardly had read an entire book of the Bible, these children sometimes knew by heart every verse of the Holy Book. Since democracy determined everything, the immigrants had done through migration and procreation what they could not achieve through force of arms centuries earlier. The other populations failed to see that everything, from Economics, Politics to International Relations and Technology served for only one purpose, the advancement of religion!

Other populations were at best described as agnostic. They believed not only in the total freedom of the individual but in his complete liberty. For instance, it was now legal in many European countries what was called Canine Cottages, studios where dog prostitutes were housed. In Brussels, Amsterdam, Paris and London, it was a thriving business for women to come have sex with dogs. The dogs were fully trained and catered for by Vets, and all this was legalized by parliaments of many nations in Europe. Ever since the fake news that a German lady Kedder gave birth to a set of puppies in Stellenbosch in Western Cape Province in South Africa, many ladies preferred to groom German Shepherd dogs as Doggies. It was now generally acceptable to switch from dating a dog to dating a guy with many ladies just simply preferring the Doggies because of fear of heartbreak. And as human beings and dogs could not procreate, this further diminished other populations.

In fact, in the last year what was trending was the House of Mammals.

It all began years earlier with a crazy idea by Rene Camus to integrate Apes more into civilization, with the popularity of the series on the Planet of Apes. A clandestine project trained the Bonobo, a class of pygmy chimpanzee with more prominent breasts than other breeds. The bonobos were trained to have sex with men since dogs could do so with ladies. After a pornographic video that went viral, showing the bonobo having an exciting sex with a man, it gradually became normal to think of such interactions.

A rich lobby group had done its homework quite well using the United Nations to advocate that it was not abnormal for a man to have sex with an animal. They came up with scientific studies that showed the benefits and the absence of any real danger. The speed with which money was put together to fast-track this campaign was amazing. If the same zeal was used in pursuing the sustainable global agenda, poverty would have ended five years earlier. Several House of Mammals (HoM) were established by law for those with such natural bestial inclinations, for many people began to realize that they were actually born with a natural orientation to have sex with animals. As a matter of fact, a new set of sexual orientation had emerged which was even taught in primary schools. It was called Bestie. Just as the world had come around to accepting gay marriages, Bestie rights was now a hot issue.

I read somewhere that secret experiments to hatch the ovaries of Apes with human spermatozoa had been carried out. Very few knew the outcome of those experiments. Nevertheless, just as there were sex toys, it was gradually becoming fashionable to have a companion bonobo. Animal rights activists had tried unsuccessfully to block the legislation citing exploitation. But judges had bought the human rights activists' viewpoint that man exercising his right to pleasure was actually socializing and dignifying the animals rather than abusing them. There was an argument about re-animalizing in place of de-animalizing.

Massachusetts was the first in the United States to pass legislation making Bestie legal and so far, more than ten states had similar legislation successfully passed. Europe had first passed cautionary measures including the fact that only those with stand-alone homes could afford to keep a Sex Ape. The rest had to go to HoMs to satiate their uncommon desires.

House of Mammals as the first-class service provider of ape coitus, had carried out extensive research on ape domestication and had identified the DNA that caused violence in apes. Through a process of conditioning they bred the bonobo for pleasure. Such female chimmos were injected with all kinds of antibiotics that killed off viruses capable of causing debilitating diseases in humans. And so many men indulged themselves and had no risk of contracting a dreaded disease. There was also no risk of getting a Bonobo pregnant or spending money on alimony. Human rights advocacy groups raised tens of millions of dollars and succeeded in fencing off conservative religious organisations.

There had been pressure from leaders of the Holy Faith on heads of government in both the UK and US to control some of these excesses but generally such advocacy had not succeeded in overturning legislation that allowed for these liberties, for it meant greater decrease in new births.

4.

I shuddered as I recalled images of the massacre that took place at the Redemption headquarters when all this exploded, how more than thirty thousand worshippers were murdered in broad daylight under television cameras in one fell swoop. It was the annual Holy Ghost convention, and because security was usually tight, the attackers knew they couldn't get in on foot. It must have been quite highly coordinated for nobody knew how they got helicopters. The attackers were dropped off by a chopper clearly marked Police. Later on, people recounted how they were fooled because 'NIGERIA' wasn't part of the inscription but simply 'POLICE'.

The chopper had hovered around for a while building the confidence of worshipers, who became momentarily distracted but thought government was taking their security quite seriously. Then in the clear sight of everyone, masked men dropped off rapidly one after another at strategic locations, bearing heavy artillery. Most worshippers who saw the operation thought the Police had tuned up its game and were probably being proactive or responding to intel, only for the five gunmen to open fire from their various locations. It was reminiscent of the Paris attacks years earlier where gun men stormed a football stadium and several bars and a theatre and killed tens of people. Recalling the Paris attacks I remembered how I missed it by a hair's breadth because I changed my ticket the previous night to return earlier from my trip rather than stay another night in Paris. It was at Heathrow that I saw footages of the attacks. I shuddered as one of the locations was where I usually went for dinner. Whereas the Paris carnage was immediately put under control, by the time the real police came with the army, the fighters of Servants of Paradise had finished off more than thirty thousand worshippers, with about five thousand more stampeded to death.

It was a gruesome sight as the images displayed on television, with the killers shouting "Allahu Akbar! Allahu Akbar!!." It was pure mayhem. I could not let out the image of the river of blood as it flickered afresh in my head even after five years, as if it just occurred.

Almost simultaneously other churches along the Ibadan Lagos expressway had come under attack, with thousands of worshipers seeing their *nunc dimitis* on that fateful Sunday. It was a bloody Sunday all around the South West, South East and the South-South, as churches in Port Harcourt, Enugu, Owerri, Abakaliki, Lagos, Calabar were attacked and thousands massacred. No one had guessed that the tribesmen who walked around as beggars, cobblers, shoe shiners, household sentries were trained to kill mercilessly. Obviously there had been a signal, for the attacks were simultaneous, all over the country, carried out by these simple looking men and completely overwhelming for the security forces who had no prior intelligence.

Meanwhile Kelechi Amadi, the first executive President of the Federal Republic of Nigeria of Igbo extraction had been held hostage by a crack team of the presidential guard loyal to SOP and Boko Haram, and was purported to have signed a surrender to the SOP commander in chief, AbdulWahab Musulimi who was now more known as AM.

You see President Buru despite his incapacitation managed to complete one term and win a second one. Though majority of people claimed to have voted for the opposition, the ruling party came off with a victory for Buru in controversial circumstances. The opposition petitioned and the case went on for three and a half years when judgment was given in favour of the opposition. Some people said it was a ploy for the north to continue ruling, because it was only left with six months to the expiration of the second term and for power to revert to the south but the court ruled in favour of the opposition and the new president had to begin his term with the oath of office and had a right to seek a second term which he got in spite of his old age, enabling the north to rule for sixteen straight years.

Buru during his first two years in office had successfully battled Boko Haram to a minimum of soft target attacks. They occasionally attacked motor parks and markets but everyone knew that their fire power had been seriously clogged. It was great relief for those in the North East as people could go about freely, as towns like Maiduguri became gradually decongested of internally displaced persons. Buru's great moment came with the return of the Potiskum girls. Of the more than two hundred girls who were abducted only 167 returned; the rest were either sold into slavery to Arab lords or vehemently refused to return after being indoctrinated with the radical ideology. The girls whom Boko Haram had allowed to escape initially were mostly those already in the faith. The ones who could not escape were the ones who needed to be taught the way of the Holy Faith. The 167 girls that returned were given back to their parents after being quarantined for several months of orientation. In one fell swoop Boko Haram and their ISWA counterparts kidnapped girls from a school in Katamkpe and promptly returned them after negotiating with the government except for a lone Christian girl. People speculated that the reason they were quick in returning the girls was because most of them were of the Holy Faith. The lone girl was reportedly stubborn and refused to renounce her faith and so did not qualify for freedom.

In the last year of Buru's first term, Boko Haram gained ascendancy, becoming quite ferocious, attacking military fortresses and making it quite impossible for the army to hold ground. They had access to stupendous amounts of ransom money and used it to buy weapons which they deployed in their offensives against the military. At some point the army was reduced to a defensive force as Boko Haram and ISWA took more of the offensive. Boko Haram and ISWA had changed tactics of holding territory and were interested mainly in making the army uncomfortable with holding territory, giving rise to their attacks against military fortresses. It was reported that sometimes they would send notices to the army of their impending invasion, and sometimes on sighting them, some chicken-hearted soldiers would abandon their posts and escape by foot to the nearest cities complaining of poor fire power in the face of more sophisticated weaponry. The terrorists enriched their armoury during these invasions, as they would seize whatever weapons they came across and sometimes captured the soldiers to teach them how to operate the weapons. Towards the election period for the second term, commanders were changed, as a north eastern governor observed that commanders from the South were better at routing Boko Haram than commanders from the North. The army was thus emboldened after the outcry from the public and from the Kanuri chieftains and began to take over the towns Boko Haram and ISWA had temporarily seized. President Abu Bakare who took over from Buru dealt decisive blows to Boko Haram and allowed them no breathing space as he did all in his power to confront them as enemies of state. Anyway, President Abu Bakare improved on Buru's record and mercilessly dealt with those who were fingered as sponsors of Boko Haram and ISWA. In his eight years of rule, there were only six attacks by the terrorists, one of which took place in the vicinity of Abuja airport without a single casualty. In his second term in office, everyone had gradually come to see the terrorists as a beheaded snake that was still kicking. But this was not before most of the villages in the North that were predominantly Christian were sacked by the terrorists, as their agenda seemed to ensure that only the Holy Faith thrived in the North.

Well-meaning Nigerians such as the Sultan of Sokoto and the Emir of Kano continued to speak against these atrocities even as they got older. Everyone took it for granted that the terrorists, like all the radical sects before them, had fizzled out and were only doing a dance of death. No one knew that they were just in hibernation. They went quiet for most of the two years that President Kelechi Amadi presided over the country, only for the well-coordinated nationwide surprise attacks on that bloody Sunday which led eventually to the capture of power by the terrorist Servants of Paradise.

I kept wondering how it was that there were no early warning signs. People lamented how plausible it was that such a grand scale operation could take place without the security forces detecting it and concluded that the security forces themselves were highly compromised.

The sheer inhumanity of the atrocities, especially with the capture and execution of President Kelechi Amadi publicly as Infidel Numero Uno, with about five Catholic Bishops and many other pastors and Bishops and the declaration of sharia rule, caused millions of Christians to just give up and embrace the terrorists' faith. Many Muslims condemned these atrocities but they were a powerless majority against a powerful minority. Security forces were put in a quandary for days and could not contain the mayhem with the superior fighting strategy of the radical fundamentalists who apparently had used the lull which confused people into thinking they had been decimated to sharpen their fighting skills. Security forces could not counter the massive offensive by the terrorists until the terrorists announced the takeover of government and the suspension of the constitution. It was a sad day for all well-meaning people in all religious and social persuasions.

5.

The Igbos around Onitsha resisted at first. They successfully repelled the combined forces of AM's SOP and other terrorists and kept vigil around both the old and the second Niger Bridge and all possible access into Onitsha. It wasn't long afterwards that the terrorist government, which had now seized the national armoury, returned with rocket launchers and destroyed many parts of Onitsha, leading to the surrender of the local populations. The terrorist government rounded up hundreds of men and made a spectacle of executing them without a choice to recant their faith. They were irked when international press, especially L'Osservatore Romano reported the deaths as martyrdom. Thenceforth they began to force people to recant the faith and forcefully convert or die.

Of course, fewer people chose death as the days went by.

Some turned to the terrorists' religion in anger. "Where was Jesus when all these things were happening?" They queried. "Where was God when all these killings were going on?"

Many others wondered at the kind of understanding of a God that celebrated such violent bloodshed just because a few deranged people wanted him to be worshipped in a particular way.

When Onitsha fell to the terrorists, Owerri and Enugu were easier targets. Only Aba proved quite tough because of the Ngwa people who were traditionally warlike but they were soon overrun. In fact, many community leaders rather began sending emissaries, asking AM and his SOP leadership to simply come and establish their authority and conduct the mass conversions rather than attack and kill. This way, towns like Ogoja, Ikom, Eket, did not witness a single gunshot. Most of the remaining populations converted to the religion of the terrorists, except for four Bishops who had managed to escape to Rome and others with their priests who were sought out and assassinated. Many pastors preached to their congregations shortly before the surrender, that it wasn't proper to 'resist the wicked', and that their members should surrender and keep the faith in their hearts. So, all over the place now, you saw young girls and women in *Hijab*. Everywhere was as quiet as a graveyard, as people learnt to worship this new way of God that invoked so much terror.

The Pope had urged world leaders to intervene. You see, after Pope Francis, Cardinal Tagle of the Philippines had shepherded the church for ten years, adopting the name Paul Vll, before Pope Augustine took over. Augustine was the very first black African Pope after more than a millennium, from Cote D'Ivoire. Though he did his best, he was not as respected as previous popes, even by his fellow Africans. The UN could not muster enough votes to mandate the Security Council to launch a military attack on the terrorist regime. The British PM, the US President, the President of France and the German Chancellor had a common history of being all sons of migrants and actively practicing a variant of the Holy faith. Although this was not much of a factor, much as they tried, a coalition that would confront the rogue regime could not be mustered. Only Russia and China made serious attempts to confront the terrorist government, although China was more interested in the economic benefits of being the largest trading partner with the terrorist government and kept saying the religious carnage was the internal affairs of Nigeria.

The UN was even in the process of reviewing the universal human rights declaration it made in 1948, the preponderant opinion being that the human rights constrained the full practice of some religions. An exceptional clause was added to accommodate religious reservations. The main target was religious liberty. Among all the fundamental human rights, it was the only one that was contentious, which then implied that it was not a priori self-evident as a right and could be left optional for nations to implement responsibly. Saudi Arabia continued to fund the construction of mosques for Muslims who were also fleeing the country because of the uncertainty. Saudi Arabia gave money to several Muslim groups in Germany, Canada, Ghana, Togo and Benin Republic to build mosques to cater for the worship needs of fleeing refugees although she didn't concede to a single church being built on Saudi soil. As secular or nonpartisan world leaders before now such as Barrack Obama, Donald Trump etc., had never raised such equity issues with Saudi Arabia, it wasn't then expected that current world leaders who were mostly Muslim descendants would ever push for such an agenda.

As a master stroke, and to be in tune with the international community AM conceded to installing the erstwhile vice President to govern as prime minister. Even though he did not subscribe to their radical brand, he was an adherent of the Holy Faith and they hoped that by Allah's will he would gradually come to accept the wisdom of such radical choices as made and imposed by Servants of Paradise. They also agreed to stop the persecution of Christians with a caveat that only those who had not converted yet would remain so, but with second class status and a special tax. In the new dispensation a non-Muslim could not superintend over the faithful. AM the Commander in Chief of the Armed Forces of the new Islamic Republic of Nigeria was also Head of State, while the former Vice President remained as head of government, in an attempt to give a humane and popular face to the murderous regime.

There had been pockets of resistances here and there in the North East and North Central of Nigeria where Christians were used to being militant but they were so summarily and mercilessly dealt with, that no one dared think of it anymore. A great many Nigerians became refugees in neighbouring countries of Cameroun, Benin Republic and as far as Ghana in a far larger scale than when the Boko Haram crisis first emanated during the President Ebeleko era. Johnson Ebeleko was a simple man from the Niger Delta who had the presidency thrust to him on a platter of gold but had no firm grip of political forces. Ebeleko had, like his acolytes, misread the situation. Being from a minority tribe, a Southerner and a Christian, his analysis of the Boko Haram threat was that it was politically motivated by those opposed to his presidency, or those using religion to express their discontent over his election. Many of his advisers also saw it as a minor threat in a region susceptible to religious radicalism and violence and believed that within a harmless space of time, the fire would be put out. Indeed, the fire was put out, with the killing of Yusuf their leader who was in incarceration. Protests mounted by members of this group were roundly decimated, with loss of lives to the membership. Then the members disappeared.

No one realized that unlike former miscreants, these ones had gone ahead to receive military training from terrorist cells in Yemen and other terrorist hubs. They developed expertise in improvised explosive devices and the handling of sophisticated military wares. Like everything Nigerian, the military generals had allowed the armed forces to rot. They embezzled the money for weapons because there was no ongoing war and invested in real estate for themselves, forgetting that an army had to be ready always to face the enemy. So, when Boko Haram became ferocious with their attacks, there was no commensurate firepower, such that they occupied a territory as large as Belgium at some point. While a soldier is his weapon, it was alleged that Nigerian soldiers could only access third grade hardware which gave up in the face of Boko Haram superior firepower. A pathetic occasion was when the military came frontally with the terrorists but their tanks could not fire because it was outdated and in disuse. Military men died in droves, some purportedly betrayed by their very commanders who were sympathetic to the cause of the radical Holy faith. When Buru took over as president and probes were carried out into security spending, it was realized that much of the security expenditure ended up in the pockets of the generals and politicians. Generals bought or built shopping malls and other multimillion-naira real estate not only in the nation's commercial and capital cities but in Dubai, London, New York. Indeed it was common knowledge that the war on Boko Haram lasted that long because it was a cash cow for those who were milking it. The capture of the Nigerian state by the SOP terrorist group and their cousins was only the natural progression.

It was amazing that issues that started as pockets of violence or disagreements could bloom so much as to consume a whole nation and a whole civilization and the religious map of Nigeria had been re-written in such a short while, the way the maps of the predominantly Christian territories of North Africa were re-written.

6.

"Hey Father."

"Hi Rust. How are you doing this evening?"

"I'm good. And you? Been watching any soccer lately?"

"Naa. My mind's off everything," I said wagging my head.

"Yeah. Isn't it a pity!"

"I know."

Rust was an 85-year-old man but quite agile. He had large palms which he boasted could slap a bear to stupor. He had worked in the coal mines in New Castle before they were closed and had huge broad shoulders. He loved moving his right fist in a soft clench, as if he was moulding a ball of *fufu*. He had a mild stroke years earlier and was used to doing that to keep his nerves active. He lived alone, just by the church. He was a great friend of Pat my colleague whom Bishop had assigned for me to live with pending the resolution of the crisis in my country. Rust never came to church to worship but occasionally he interacted with us whenever we came across him cutting his lawn or doing some manual work.

"It's a pity such a massacre is still going on in your country. I saw that they beheaded four priests yesterday who had been in hiding."

"Yeah I saw that too. Horrible."

"What sort of God requires such heinous acts from worshippers?" he shrugged his shoulders.

"I think it's more an understanding of God, their understanding of God. I believe the real God is kind and merciful. God is love. But I think their understanding is that he is a sadist who enjoys seeing blood spilled all over the place. So, they go to kill on his behalf."

"But even if they think such a God is crazy, can't they be reasonable? Why can't they realize that taking innocent lives isn't right?" Rust queried.

"You see they first get indoctrinated. They are first taught as kids that the other is worthless. They grow with that mindset. A goat is more valued than an infidel. And when you are slaughtering a goat you don't go considering its extended family. In fact, it is worst, because the infidel is seen more like a pest. And who gives a thought when killing a mosquito? It all begins from what we teach them when they are young."

For a moment Rust considered what I said in silence. My mind too cast quickly to the North East of Nigeria with the phenomenon we called the Almajiri. In the core North of Nigeria, many parents simply gave birth to droves of children and handed them over to religious teachers to educate and fend for, and as the teachers had no means of livelihood, the daily routine of the children was to go around with plates begging for food and money, accompanied by a host of flies and fleas amidst stinking breath and unwashed odoriferous bodies. These children would have only Arabic education and if they learnt any skills, it would be shoe mending and shoe shining and all such sundry stuff. They were neither gainfully employed nor employable as their only exposure was to Arabic and religious education. They were made to believe that as deep as they were in their situation, they were better than even a Senator of the federal republic if the senator was of another faith. Northern elites and state governments did very little to implement the universal basic education, and most of these boys accounted for the millions of out-of- school children Nigeria boasted of. And yet they served a great purpose! As thugs during political campaigns, as spearheads during religious riots, as under age voters during elections; they were the prime recruits as fighters during any form of jihad because with a free plate of food, they could maim and kill. The political elites kept them uneducated to serve that purpose of advancing their agenda because these tykes had no care for their lives nor the lives of others. Their lives were already a martyrdom, except that they were like an elephant run amok in a china shop because they did not live their lives to die alone but to bring other souls along with theirs, the souls of the infidels whom they were saving from a depraved life by killing them. So, when the all-out jihad broke out, these children who had become grown men and scattered all over the country as shoe shiners, as night sentry men, were the ones who led the individualized breakout squads springing surprises and overwhelming the entire nation. And it all had to do with what they were told when they were young, to resent the other, to look down and consider the other as worse than phlegm that is spat out, or as the noisy anopheles sought for a kill with a clap of the hands.

"You are right," he said, rubbing his hand on the shovel. "The world will never be rid of radicalism as long as there are holy texts promoting the violent suppression of others."

"Well, I am not sure we can get rid of any holy texts. I mean if they are holy, they are holy. But we can help with how we look at what they tell us to do. We can have a better understanding of them. You know there was a time the Catholic Church held that the Bible was a literal and historical text. So, if the Bible said the four corners of the earth, no scientist could say the earth was spherical and remain alive. If the Bible said the earth was the center of the universe, no scientist could say the sun was the center of the solar system and still be breathing. But then the church embraced science. Scientific ways of reading literary texts were applied to the scriptures and it was discovered that you could separate what was a myth from a mystery or a revealed truth."

"Yeah I agree with you. You Catholics used to burn people at the stake. Galileo escaped being burnt. And now the Catholic church is a promoter of science! But surely such things as Jesus dying and resurrecting are no scientific facts!"

"Well, except in the sense that history is not an exact science, because Jesus' death and Resurrection is a historical reality."

"Oh yeah ?"

"Of course Rust. There is no doubt that Jesus walked this earth, died, and resurrected. What we make of that is part of the mystery of our faith which comes from revealed truth. Scientific truths are not the only truths. Revealed truths, mysteries beyond human comprehension are true nonetheless. If there is anything that cannot be untrue in the entire Bible, it is the fact that Jesus Christ died and rose from the dead. But things like Adam eating an apple given by a snake to his wife are myths. These were teaching methods of the ancients and all they wanted to say was that God made the world and made it good but it was corrupted by our fore parents who were misled by Satan."

"I hope you do realize, that Jesus' redemptive act is a function of that happenstance between Adam and Eve?" Rust asked with a quizzical smirk.

"Of course, I do. Actions have consequences, and sometimes very little actions have enduring consequences. Certainly, the choices of the progenitors of humanity led to negative consequences which God intervened to reverse through Jesus Christ, and to offer him as a constant source of hope and dignity. However we came to the downside as a human family, Jesus Christ has brought us back to the upside. I wished all faiths could separate what is truly salvific from what is exclusive and damning."

"Did you see the picture of the failed suicide bomber who wore armour protecting his penis?" he said laughing almost uncontrollably.

I laughed too. "Yeah I saw that."

When the young man was interviewed he claimed he

was protecting his penile members from shattering so he would be able to have sex with the 72 virgins when he eventually met with them as gifts from the Holy Prophet in Paradise.

"So, is it all about sex? I mean, you kill a thousand people and kill yourself so you could have sex with virgins forever in paradise?" He wasn't laughing anymore and was for a second deep in thought, scratching his head. "Maybe sex is paradise, you know. Then why not just have it here at once. I mean it's so cheap anyone can buy it. You don't need to have known anyone beforehand. Why not have your fucking paradise right here instead of having to kill others and yourself first?" I made a soft whine and wagged my head. "You know that is why I don't go to church. I can't understand why we could be so advanced in technology, why we could be so educated and yet so backward in our reasoning in the name of faith. It beats my imagination. I could never understand how God would order the Israelites to destroy other tribes and take possession of their lands. I couldn't understand those massacres in the Bible. And who knows, that is what these terrorists are claiming. You Christians celebrate these atrocious Jewish stories as your scripture, the massacre of innocent people in ancient times and the forceful takeover of their territories and you want me to come and worship your God. These terrorists are no different, they believe their God has given them a mandate to slaughter everyone who does not want to embrace their brand of faith." He concluded with a contemptuous pout.

7.

For a moment I was taken aback by his vehemence. It was so easy to take it for granted that people understood these matters without realizing that they were a stumbling block to the faith of many. How would I go about explaining that as much as these were revealed texts, they were not a dictation but accommodated anthropomorphisms, where the human agent acted according to his level of socialization and sometimes wrote of the divine from his human understanding? But then just as the Israelites believed that God had given them the land of Canaan, in the 21st century, the Fulani believed that Allah had given them the land called Nigeria, and their militant squads had no qualms going in the dead of night, killing everyone in their sight including pregnant women and children in a bid to take over ancestral lands belonging to communities in the middle belt. Buru had made attempts to allocate lands for them in all the states of the federation but backed down because of the outcry by Nigerians at such open state support for an ethnic agenda. The militants had therefore intensified their invasion of communities not just in the middle belt but in the South-West and South-South of Nigeria, slaughtering, burning down, displacing whole communities believing it was their divine right, until Abubakare came and restored some degree of sanity, only for a more serious carnage to erupt a few years later.

"Rust, believe me. Things have changed. That was their understanding of the Divinity. The Divinity doesn't change but our understanding changes, it grows with time, with more knowledge and insight. Can't you see? From an understanding of a God who was exclusively theirs, the Jews came to know that he was God for all the nations. And about those conquests, that is how things worked in those days, not just among the Jews. You had your European wars. We had our inter-tribal wars. It was might as right. If you were stronger, you went on military expeditions and took over territories and either killed them or made them vassals. That is how it worked for centuries until nation states emerged and boundaries were fixed and citizens entered into social contracts with the State and various states made pacts amongst themselves until the emergence of the United Nations. Some religions did spread through these kinds of conquests because it was the methodology of that time. I mean there was a time human beings owned others as property! There was a time a king could give orders for someone to be slain for doing nothing, remember how Herod killed babies because he was jealous? Can you imagine that it was only in 1948 that there was a universal declaration of human rights? 1948 Rust! 1948. Things have changed. Territories are pretty much defined. No one can use the argument of what happened then to apply now."

"History is repetitive you know," Rust said with a frown. "What has happened once can happen again."

I was quiet for a moment considering what he had said *What has happened once can happen again!*

"You are right Rust. And we have an ever weakened United Nations Systems. But you know what? I think that in the final analysis Jesus the Christ has come to throw great light on our relationships, that God indeed is love, and that everyone is your neighbor because everyone is a child of God. Even if nothing else, we need to amplify that understanding of good neighborliness, that I could be different, I could worship differently or not worship at all like you Rust, but you are my neighbour. A common humanity should teach us about a common God no matter what format we worship him."

"I guess you are right. But I still can't understand how a man drives his car onto a pedestrian walkway and kills innocent people in the name of his God." Rust was referring to a terror attack that took place in August 2018 in Westminster. A British man that was originally from another country drove a silver coloured Ford Fiesta from Birmingham in the middle of the night to London and committed the havoc the following morning by driving onto the opposite direction and swerving onto cyclists and pedestrians in Parliament Square and injuring a few persons. And then in Nice, South of France, a holiday town, a man drove a truck into a crowd of people and killed several. Ever since security forces stepped up their act on arresting suspects and monitoring arms and potential weapons, terrorists had become innovative in weaponing every day facilities and utilities. Then in November 2019 a supposed rehabilitated terrorist stabbed two person on London Bridge.

"Me neither," I said, looking at my watch. Rust was a great conversationalist and you could spend the whole day with him without being bored as he seemed to be quite acquainted with a number of subjects. But you had to be careful to know when to cut him off. My strategy was to look at my watch as a sign that time was running out. "Seriously Rust, I can't seem to get what makes them so angry, so restless, so violent. My consolation is that they are quite few, they are a tiny minority. The rest of the believers are law abiding and accommodating."

"Bullshit." Rust said, his face turning red apparently in hot emotion. "It's not crowds that make inventions. Two men with enough ammunition can finish off a million defenseless people. It doesn't have to be a majority. The tiniest minority can cause all the good which all could benefit. And so is their ability to cause evil. During Stalin's time the majority counted for nothing, during Hitler's time, the majority of Germans counted for nothing when the Nazis killed 6 million Jews, the Soviet revolution took more than 20 million lives with the majority not being able to do anything; the Chinese communist revolution took more than 70 million lives with the majority of the people not able to do anything or is it the Japanese who murdered more than 12 million people in Asia before World War ll? And your country too, before now it gained a reputation for cybercrime, but how many Nigerians were engaged in it? The tiny powerful minority determine the way a group or a culture is looked at my friend."

"I guess you are right." I looked at my watch again.

"I mean look at it. Yes, majority are peace loving and law abiding but why is it that 99% of terrorists come from their fold?"

"Rust I know a few men and boys that have walked into schools, shopping malls and mosques and killed innocent people and they did not shout Allahu Akbar…" I was talking of the Far-Right terrorist groups and individuals.

"I know. I know. Those are far flung cases, persons with unhinged minds."

"No Rust. The Far-Right is as much a threat as those radical fundamentalists."

"True maybe. But these guys, their culture seems to be like an active volcano. No matter how peaceful a volcano appears to be, it is in its DNA to erupt and spread molten."

"But volcanos are made to erupt. It is natural," I said laughing at the example.

"Precisely. In this case it is cultural. We have to accept the reality that, no matter how it is dressed, this is a religion that fundamentally does not accept the freedom of others to worship God the way they want and has fertile grounds to breed few but powerful adherents who would always interpret things in a violent way. The world has to accept that reality and live with it. It only gets worse when the religion mixes up in an environment that has an *honor* culture."

"Perhaps you have a point Rust, I mean this last point you made about honor; because in my country the South Western part had a great number of people practicing different religions and living peacefully. In many cases the husband lived conveniently with his wife who was of another faith and even allowed the children to be of her faith. The children grew up celebrating the major feasts of all the religions in their homes. But this was never the practice in the North East and North West who have honor cultures. It would be a thing of shame and they would rather die than live with it. True I am beginning to think rather that this is more a matter of culture than doctrine. In the South West, they are Yorubas before being religious or anything else but in the North East and North West they are religious before being Hausa or Fulani and their honor culture seems to tailor towards assuaging that identity whether in politics, economics or social policy. In fact, we say in my country that the northerners don't regard the South West Yoruba as religious enough."

I looked at my watch again.

"Oh really?"

"Oh yes. So, I guess if the English embraced the religion it would be different, won't it? Because then your values of tolerance and politeness would come into its practice."

"I guess so. But let's just say that the failure of the state accounts for any festering of any form of violence, whether merely economic or political riots, or even religious. A strong state with effective institutions would maintain the monopoly of the instruments of violence and would not allow miscreants to hold it hostage in whatever name. That is what happened in your country. Your government lost it to the terrorists from the beginning and this is the consequence. Over here state institutions are alert and respond immediately to all security issues. But it looks like your government allowed the child to grow into a man before attempting to nurture him. Doesn't work that way. Guess you need to go. Have a good one. Talk some other time," he said and made to bend down to continue with his work as I looked at my watch again.

"Thanks a lot Rust. It was really nice sharing with you. I am quite relieved. This means a lot. Actually, I want to get some groceries across the street for dinner. My colleague is waiting."

"Great. See you another time then. You could stop by for a cuppa you know."

"Thanks Rust. I should."

8.

I first stopped to get Coffee mate at the corner shop. I was in Carshalton Beeches in Surrey, under the Archdiocese of Southwark, at St. Margaret of Scotland Roman Catholic Church. It was a sleepy outskirt of a town a little more than an hour from London. A Nigerian priest was the pastor in the church. We were mates in school and he had chosen after twenty years of serving in Nigeria to migrate to the UK and incardinate into the diocese. He had been on mission for only three years when he was persuaded to remain behind and incardinate. I was just in residence and had no pastoral responsibilities apart from what he assigned to me. Of course, as a priest I had to celebrate the Eucharist everyday so I had to be in church.

I filed officially to be recognized as a refugee though I had a valid visitor's visa for ten years. My visa would not allow me extend my stay beyond six months at a time so I had to file for special status. I would have gone back if it were possible and I really felt sad that I could not. British Airways had suspended all flights to the country after the terrorists downed a plane, killing all 268 passengers and crew. The country had become a pariah state, although the terrorist government was doing its best to reverse the status.

"You don't seem to have any Coffee mate around," I said as I scanned the corner shop.

"No, we don't. You may have to go down to Tesco."

"Thanks."

"How's the situation in your country man?"

"We're still watching."

"I read this morning that the Niger Delta Resistance Army has taken over Port Harcourt. I have been following events there."

"Oh. Well…I don't know where that would lead to anyways. I am just so fed up with all the confusion," I said and bade him a good day. Like most of the store attendants, he was Asian. Like everyone else, he knew I was Nigerian and Nigeria was always up in the news with updates of atrocities by the 'holy' regime; so those with any acquaintances always wanted to share banters.

I walked listlessly to Tesco and got the stuff I needed. I went to the kitchen and washed the plates before putting them into the dish washer. I mopped the floor. Fr. Pat my host teased me that I was useless domestically so I tried to demonstrate some value. Over time I had gotten used to their style. Back in Nigeria we had domestic staff doing everything from cleaning to cooking to serving. Here you were your chef, laundry man, steward, driver, sacristan, because labour was expensive. I could not cook really, so I tried to help with the preparation of the condiments each time Pat wanted to cook. It was a double effort for him at first since I did not enjoy his vegetable diets and he had to make something I could eat as well. He was heavily built with broad shoulders that gave him out as a sportsman in his early years. Over time he had slacked and put on a lot of weight which he now tried to trim through dieting and long walks. Since I joined him I had been initiated into the long walks. Nearly twenty years earlier when I first visited him, we took a walk after lunch in these quiet streets and came across a police van. I gave no thought to it until Pat said, "Those Police officers are watching us. Guess they are wondering what two black men are doing in a white neighbourhood on a lonely afternoon." There was not a soul on the road. They drove slowly past us. "I bet you. They will come back this way," he said. "And they might chat with us to know what we are up to." "That'll be interesting." I said. Luckily, we saw one of Pat's parishioners, who just happened to open her door to step outside. Pat went over to chat with her while I stood across the road. After a few minutes, true to Pat's prediction, the police van drove on the crescent and came past us again. Of course, they saw Pat chatting and laughing with the old white lady. That was a sign that we were part of the neighborhood. They drove off.

"See what I told you? They came back. This is what I call security! You engage in surveillance, you watch out for the early warning signs and nip them in the bud. You don't allow a situation to escalate out of control."

"I thought you were concerned about the stereotype of black and criminal."

"That is immaterial for now," he said.

9.

As I remembered the conversation its import hit me afresh and tears welled up in my eyes. A good security force would have identified the issues from the onset of Boko Haram and dealt with them decisively and comprehensively. A good government would force children to go to school so they don't become a ready army conscripted through a promise of a daily meal. A conscientious leadership would work to eliminate all those inequalities that bred rascals, although the experience of the UK and other parts of Europe showed that even in societies where there were social safety nets, youths were still radicalized. The internet had become radicalism-made-easy, but even if one were to fix all the underlying issues, what do you do with a man who believes that to have sex in paradise he must bring a hundred heads as booty? Should not all religions respect the fundamental rights of others to exist at least? Couldn't rational men and women in each religion come together and de-emphasize what demeaned other human beings in the worship of their God? If perchance a God demanded obnoxious things in the past because of overriding circumstances then, couldn't rational men just plainly see that enough was enough and we had gone past the Amalekites and Jebusites? And if the state that should guarantee the rights of all became the instrument of propagation of terrorism what hope was there for co-existence?

I went upstairs to get Pat. Everything was ready for the vegetable stew.

"Can you imagine?" He said, his eyes still fixed on the magazine.

"No, I can't," I joked. "What is it?"

"There is an article urging Rome to allow a Rite of Union for Besties."

"Holy Moses! They want to make Catholics of Chimps?" I exclaimed, laughing.

"My dear it's not a laughing matter o. This is how it starts and before you know it some people will start bringing their pets for baptism."

I laughed.

"But Christ died for the whole of creation," I said. "Even animals should be saved."

"I hope you are not a Bestie," he said jocularly. We laughed it off.

How differently our times had become. All the

advances in science and technology, all the knowledge replete in the internet, and yet a dark age understanding of religion! History was a cycle. Who would believe that this was the 21st Century?

10.

Months passed.

I never saw Rust to accept his invitation for a cup of tea. I didn't think it was appropriate to just bump into someone's house without notice. Back in Nigeria I could do that and present no offence but here someone might even call the police for me. There was something ominous about his absence. It was strange that the last conversation we had was the last time I set my eyes on him. I decided to ask Pat. His eyes were fixed on his laptop. He scarcely raised his head as he spoke to me.

"Oh, I thought I mentioned it. Rust was rushed to the hospital for heart surgery. He didn't make it. He's already been cremated."

"What!"

"I am sorry. I really thought I mentioned it. I wouldn't have known myself but for the after mass coffee one of those weekdays. Parishioners were talking about it. You probably were not in church that day."

I felt really sad. I was not sure I would have attended the funeral but to have died for over two months and the fact unknown to me was terrible. It was typical here, that the silent streets held lots of news which you only knew if you asked or were at the right place at the right time.

"Oh, my Lord!" Pat exclaimed suddenly.

"What is it again?" I shined down the stairs as I was

on the landing and leaning on the railing.

"Can you imagine this! The Pope has accepted the invitation of the rogue regime to visit Nigeria!"

"That is not possible."

"But here it is. This is the Vatican website. L'Osservatore Romano."

Quickly I went through the news item. "Are you sure it is the official site? Remember that during Pope Francis' time many people opened various fake websites and fake Facebook accounts and were writing nonsense and attributing to the Pope, some quite contrary to Catholic teaching?"

"My dear I am sure the news is real. Take a look yourself."

We sat back talking about the planned trip of the Pope. Was it not a misadventure? How did the regime even initiate such an idea or was it the idea of the Pope himself? As a child the Pope had been born to Muslim parents who died in his country's civil uprising. He was adopted by a family and educated by a Christian family. Naturally he had to join the foster parents to church and expressed interest quite early in the reading of the Bible. He trained as a cyber-engineer before receiving the call to train as a priest and held two doctoral degrees in Islam and in sacred scripture which he taught in the regional seminary before being made bishop, and Archbishop and Cardinal. He could speak Arabic, French, Italian, English, Spanish and his native Yakouba. Had he communicated with them in a way they understood and wanted to hear him out? Was it that they were tired of their pariah status and wanted to show the world that they were open to dialogue? Or was it a ploy to openly assassinate the Pope in the view of television cameras all over the world, being that it was a core hope of Islamic radicals to behead the Pope publicly at St. Peter's Square with the prospect of frightening the whole world into submission to their religion? But then how would the head of a state no matter how rogue he might be invite a prominent citizen of the world in order to behead him? Wouldn't that lead to a major crisis in the world? Except that the rogue regime was married to controversy already and even if an atomic bomb shattered them to electrons, neutrons and protons, they would die happily, knowing that they had achieved the greatest desire of their radical faith.

There was a frenzy all over the world all of a sudden especially on social media, much more than when Donald Trump the 45th president of the United States decided to have a summit with Kim Jong-Un in 2018. CNN had already scheduled a panel discussion that morning, with majority of the discussants giving thumps down to the visit. One even alleged that the Pope was using the visit to score a popularity and relevance point since he had not been as influential as his predecessors while one discussant opined that it might be good for the US marines to accompany the pope. A few outrageous social media commentators were even alleging that having been born Muslim and having studied Islam to doctoral level the pope was finally going to Nigeria to abdicate and re-embrace his true religion. Apparently, US intelligence had got whiff of this trip much earlier for later that evening the Secretary of State announced that the US military would begin an exercise to flush out pirates in the Gulf of Guinea and the activities coincided with the planned visit of the Pope to Nigeria. A week later the

UN Security Council issued a warning that were anything to happen to the Pope as head of the Vatican State, the world body would not sit by and watch. Everyone was suddenly concerned.

We all waited, counting the days which were only three weeks away. Many more discussions were held, some predicting already what the pope was going to say or suggesting what he should say since it had become inevitable that he must attend. Some wondered whether he would be bold enough to condemn the brutality of the regime frontally or whether such messages would be drowned in convoluted insinuations. Diaspora Nigerian Catholics were urging the Pope to visit Nigeria as a miracle could occur much as it happened during the visit of Pope John Paul ll to Nigeria in March 1998 during the repressive regime of General Sani Abacha. Pope John Paul ll had visited Nigeria for the canonization of Blessed Tansi and was a guest of the Head of State General Sani Abacha. The Pope urged the general to release political prisoners chief of whom were MKO Abiola and Olusegun Obasanjo. Abacha died three months later in June, without freeing the prisoners. It was speculated then that it was because he reneged on his promise to the Pope that he died suddenly. Diaspora Nigerians were thus hoping that an angel of death might accompany the Pope on his visit with AM.

CNN went back to the archives to review what Pope John Paul ll said then at the meeting with the Muslim community in Nigeria, observing that the situation now was quite different.

All of us, Christians and Muslims, live under the sun of the one merciful God. We both believe in one God who is creator of

Man. We acclaim God's sovereignty and we defend man's dignity as God's servants. We adore God and profess total submission to him. Thus, in a true sense, we can call one another brothers and sisters in faith in the one God. And we are grateful for this faith, since without God the life of man would be like the heavens without the sun.

Because of this faith we have in God, Christianity and Islam have many things in common: the privilege of prayer, the duty of justice accompanied by compassion and almsgiving, and above all a sacred respect for the dignity of man, which is at the foundation of the basic rights of every human being including the right to life of the unborn child…

That speech was years before 9/11, before the consciousness of everyone was awakened to the fact that apart from race, religion could be such an instrument of violence, repression and mass murder. Overnight religion escalated mutual suspicions and prejudices worldwide and ragtag as well as well-trained armies sprung up all over the world to enforce hate, turning once peaceful nations to shadows of themselves and once noble citizens into 'dregs of humanity'. The only upside to it was the improvement in travel security. Would the current Pope's message be as inclusive as that of John Paul ll? would it go to great lengths to show that what was common was much more than what was different?

11.

The D-Day came with an anti-climax.

I got called to an urgent sick-call. As a priest, a sick-call was one thing you did not mess with, you had to abandon everything and attend to it. I tried my best to maintain a stoical disposition as the poor woman that came to pick me obviously did not know how important the Pope's visit to my country was. It would have been nice to get it firsthand but I knew that the major cable networks and of course the online media would splash everything in a split second all over the web so I did my best to be attentive to my mission to the sick. The terrorist regime had opened access to online media after they had locked the country out for more than four years. I was grateful I responded to the call, for the woman died right in my presence after hearing her confession and giving her Holy Communion. These were moments that were not sensational but really great for a priest. Being by the side of someone who really needed you was a great thing.

I returned just in time to catch a glimpse of the Pope's address to the religious scholars. Scholars had been invited from Egypt, Saudi Arabia, Thailand, Iran and several other nations, as the Pope wanted to use the occasion for a dialogue with fellow Islamic scholars. I stood with my mouth agape.

"...*You believe and worship God who is omnipotent, benevolent and merciful and so indeed He is. But why do allow a tiny minority to define your religion as far removed from a merciful and benevolent God ?...*" He went on to reiterate the fact that majority of people identify with a particular faith because they were born into it and no one should be blamed for practicing a particular religion, that the primary thing is that we are first of all human before we discover we are religious and therefore one humanity; that God is a mystery whom no one could understand fully and therefore human beings were not qualified to talk about God in such a way as if they were the only ones that could understand who God is. That if indeed God is

Almighty, as indeed He was, human beings were powerless to fight God or fight for God; that powerful men in times past had seen religion as a tool for control and so used it to control others into submission but that it was now time to be reasonable. *"Search your scriptures and reverence what was useful in the past but practice only that which aligns with natural justice, that which is reasonable and respects the life and dignity of others. Be reasonable. Respect life as a gift from God. Terminating any life, even your own is not God's will. Be reasonable… Teach your children to love not only their kind but all humanity. For religion is not a contest between our various understanding of God but a way of the soul's journey to the divine. There is only one God. The way of violence is never the way of God…"*

Then the pope launched off script into Arabic for about five minutes, speaking rapidly. Soon CNN brought in English translation voice-over and we could only catch the last of the sentences. *"…No merciful God will order anyone to shed innocent blood on his behalf. Go back and take control from the anarchists. Go back and begin to teach the young that there is one God but various understanding of the One God… Go back and teach people to repent and be reasonable. Repent and practice peace…"*

It was not known whether any of the papal officials had any prior knowledge of what he was going to say but for a Pope, the message was unimaginably and unexpectedly direct. What got into him to speak like that? Righteous anger? The Holy Spirit? And yet it was the truth everyone was afraid to tell because of political correctness. Some analysts said the radical fundamentalists constituted about 20% of the total population of the religion, which was a population larger than several countries put together; these radicals had a burning passion to bring down civilization as we knew it, to entrench a dark age of ruthlessness under the guise of entrenching strict moral codes, with the majority of the peaceful adherents of the religion quite helpless and redundant. It was the fastest growing religion no doubt but the radicals were not depending on divine power to grow it, they were desperate canvassers of a worldview where intimidation, exploitation, violence, treachery, oppression, domination, manipulation was fair game as long as it promoted their cause.

CNN provided translation of what the Pope had said earlier in Arabic and it had to do with his appealing to the scholars to organize themselves into a central teaching authority which would harmonize the teaching of the religion with the best of what was human, advising for a new list of Fatwas which recognized the rights of every one to worship and which denounced and renounced violence and any compulsion in religion. I was not sure how far that would go. The very fact that it was coming from the head of a major Christian denomination might make it unacceptable and even if it was it would take years for it to become the culture and there would always be some social condition that would trigger radicalization since western civilization had come to be seen by those religious radicals as synonymous with Christianity even when western cultures had all become secular and anti-theistic and Christians had become a minority; yet whatever was done in national interest by western nations was still seen as having Christian undertones and therefore worthy of condemnation and violent reprisal!

Maybe Rust's postulation was the way forward. With

some conditions there was nothing really you could do about eliminating them other than to manage them. There was nothing anyone could do about a volcano. You just learnt to live with it until it erupted and exhausted its molten magma. It would be essential to monitor and prepare for an eruption but you couldn't stop a volcano from being a volcano no matter the length of years it was inactive. Nation states could strengthen their systems and institutions to prevent and deal with organized ideologically driven destructs but it was no guarantee that ideologues would not emerge from some sect or from the far right, fly away with a verse of radical scripture or radical philosophy and consolidate and cause mayhem.

All I was wishing for was to go home. Some of my extended family had escaped into the Cameroons and had been in touch. My village now had an Imam and my local government had an Emir and almost everyone had capitulated. The local church was now a mosque, complete with minarets. If we had believed the signs, if we had not taken things for granted, if the West had not been silenced and their eye balls splashed and blinded by oil money, if they had not lost the faith and become indifferent, all these would not have happened, and now here I was, a helpless fugitive of conscience.

12.

I woke up with a start.

I was drenched in sweat. I felt quite weak. My joints were painful. My heart was pounding. Suddenly it struck me that I had been dreaming. So, this was all a nightmare! Oh my! Oh my! Thank God!

Or was it a vision?

Had I been given a vision of what might happen if non-state groups got too powerful? Or was it a vision of an inevitability? Was Nigeria on a time bomb?

And how mysterious it was, that in a duration of nine hours of sleep I had gone through a span of years. Was this how eternity was, life and years flying by unlocked by a moment of sleep?

I would really need to treat this suspected malaria first.

ABOUT THE AUTHOR

Evaristus Agbisong Bassey is a Catholic priest. He is author of a collection of short stories entitled *The Proposal and Other Stories*; and a novel titled *The Young Cleric*. He did literary studies at the University of Calabar Nigeria and the Goldsmith University of London. *Loaves of Bodies* is his third literary publication. He is author also of Localizing A Global Agenda, and Issues in Church and Society.

9 789978 573187 3